Mad World:
EPIDEMIC

Samaire Provost

ISBN: 147831737X
ISBN-13: 978-1478317371

Mad World:
EPIDEMIC

Samaire Provost

For Stephen, for giving me the chance.

CONTENTS

All myths have a basis in fact

Chapter One

Zombies. Who knew? No one. In early 2012, scientists at Stanford University in Palo Alto, California, began to recreate the microbe that had caused the Black Death in 14th century Europe. They were successful. They awoke this deathly illness, and then it jumped to modern times, and they discovered some details not previously known. There was a reason those mass graves were so hastily dug, so quickly filled. There was a reason the sickness spread so quickly, a reason so many died. Stanford's team couldn't have known that the microbe's virulence would be impossible to contain.

But I jump ahead of myself. The Stanford scientists were in the middle of their experiments when my Advanced Acting class at Bullard High began planning our year-end senior trip to NYC. It was April of 2012, and six of us had been chosen to make the trip east. By the time we had flown across the country, seen our Broadway Play and toured the Big Apple, Stanford was already well on its way to dooming our country, and eventually, the entire world. I wrote down everything that happened, so that there would be a record of how the world went mad. My name is Alyssa Gonzalez, and this is our story.

We first heard about the emergency about the same time it was leaked to the rest of the country. It was pretty late in the evening, and we had all settled down after a day of sightseeing.

"Coach Turner says nobody can be reached in Palo Alto at all," I overheard the conversation coming from the boys' room as I passed down the hall. Hurrying to the room I shared with Caitlin and Emily at the far end of the corridor, worry burned in my chest.

"Emily, have you got a signal yet?" I asked as I burst into our room. Emily was 17 and a tiny, slight Japanese girl with short black hair, dark brown eyes, and an infectious laugh. Her size was deceptive: she was an excellent actress and friend, plus she was so sweet that everyone loved her. She volunteered on weekends at our local animal shelter, walking the dogs and spending time with the other animals to socialize and keep them from going nuts in their ridiculously small cages.

"No signal. Calls aren't going through," Emily said.

Caitlin had switched on the room's TV set and was listening intently. "Shhh! There's something on about the blackout in California!" she hissed. Caitlyn was the friend who could win 'Most likely to save the planet.' She was an earth child, very into saving the planet and not ruining the environment. She had long, thick brown hair and brown eyes and favored blue jean and T-shirts about skirts and sandals. A girl after my own heart. I also lived in blue jeans and T-shirts.

I was the ringleader in our group of friends. I'd excelled in our debate and speech classes and last fall was voted class president of our school. Some people might have called me bossy; I preferred to think of myself as decisive. I took after my grandfather, Miguel Gonzalez, who owned several businesses in town. *Casa de Sabores*, which my mother managed, was the best Mexican restaurant in the valley and was my grandfather's biggest business. Abuelo also owned two dry cleaners. His son, my father, was stationed in Afghanistan and had been for six months. We missed him terribly. Captain Gonzalez was expected home in two months, and I couldn't wait.

We all huddled around the TV.

"No word yet on what exactly is going on in California. The government has grounded all flights and trains to the area," the announcer said. "The president is expected to make an announcement in a few moments."

We paused expectantly.

Minutes later, President Obama appeared behind a desk.

"Good evening, ladies and gentlemen. Minutes ago, I finished conferring with my team and I have news regarding the events in central California. Scientists at Stanford University in Palo Alto have had a breach of a highly sensitive, highly contagious microbe from their lab. The entire area has been sealed. No air traffic is allowed near the containment site. As we speak, troops from all over the Southwest are converging on the area. Marines from Camp Pendleton have already arrived."

"What?" said Caitlin, nervously running her fingers through her hair. "They got there already? That base is a day from Palo Alto. This happened earlier?"

"Shhh!"

As if anticipating our questions, the president continued:

"The timeline for these events began late last night. I was informed of the breach in the early hours of the morning. I immediately dispatched our soldiers to the area to lock it down, to avoid spread of this deadly contagion." The president continued. "Please be calm and stay patient. We ask that you not travel into the central valley region of California until the crisis is averted."

"Well, that's easy for him to say!" Emily whispered. Our families all lived in Fresno. Our acting class was from Bullard High School. This year-end trip with our acting coach was supposed to be a treat. Now all we could think of was our families back home.

"I am not staying here while my mom and brother are in possible danger," I said shakily.

"Yeah, me neither," said Emily. "Let's go ask Coach Turner what the plan is."

We got up and hurried down the hall to the room where the boys from our class were staying. The door stood open. As we entered, we saw Coach Turner and all the guys huddled around their room's TV too. We gathered around them, watching the set for any new information. The president just repeated the earlier warning we'd heard in our room.

Turner mumbled, "Dear God…" and turned down the sound on the set. "Guys, we don't exactly know what they're dealing with. The government wants us all to sit tight where we are. But I've got my wife and twins out there back in Fresno and I have to think about what I'm going to do. Has anyone been able to get a cell phone call through yet?"

Everyone shook their heads no.

"Well, keep trying. Meanwhile, I've got some ideas. Can you kids stay here while I go and check around?"

Coach Turner had been our acting teacher for the last two years. He had done some acting in Hollywood and then turned to teaching when the supporting roles in which he was cast failed to pay the rent. His wildly curly brown hair, framing a round face, was a familiar sight on campus. He had also coached girls volleyball for the past eight years, and was a much loved figure at our school.

"Coach, what do you have in mind?" Jacob asked. Jake was a tall 18-year-old who I'd known since grade school. His light brown hair and green eyes had captured my notice back in junior high. Unfortunately, it had also caught the eyes of a lot of other girls, too. Jake, being the strong, silent type, had basically ignored this female attention and hunkered down, concentrating on his studies. He was a straight-A student and a member of the track team.

Since I'd turned 17 last fall, I'd sort of blossomed, thank goodness. I was tired of being the Plain Jane type I'd been in my preteen years. With longer hair, and my maturing, both physically and mentally, I'd come into my own. I hoped Jake had noticed.

My attention was pulled from contemplating Jacob to Coach, who was talking again.

"I'm going to try to get us some kind of transportation," Turner said. "If they're not allowing flights in, maybe we can at least get close to our families by land. And I need to get to an ATM." He checked his cell phone. "Listen, it's almost 7 p.m. I don't want any of you wandering around at night in this city. Just hang tight, order some room service, and wait for me. OK? I shouldn't be more than a couple of hours."

"Yeah."

"Okay."

"You got it, Coach," said Conner, a muscular African-American weightlifter who had decided to try acting junior year and realized he loved it. Conner had lost his father, a police officer, the year he turned ten, and ever since then he'd been determined to follow in his footsteps and enter the Police Academy. He was on the track team with Jacob and they had a friendly rivalry going at each track meet. He favored black and red cross trainers and jackets that matched and had dark eyes and very dark, ebony skin, which the girls loved. Unfortunately, he had no interest in them at all, and neither did his boyfriend Charles.

Turner got up, grabbed his jacket and room key, and hurried out. Before the hotel room door completely shut, he stuck his head in again. "And keep the door locked, you hear me? People tend to go a little nuts during emergencies. You've got to stay safe." Then he exited the room, shutting the door firmly behind him.

"Man, this is scary," said DeAndre, a tall and gangly senior who might have qualified as the class clown. You know how they call people characters? DeAndre was a character, and a character actor, as well. He usually played supporting roles in our class productions, but he also frequently stole the show. DeAndre's short curly brown hair and warm smiling brown eyes, and his bright smile and easy manner had captured plenty of female attention. His complexion was lighter than Conner's, because D's mom was white.

"It will be okay. Coach will take care of us. We just have to sit tight and wait for him," said Jake. He smiled to reassure us.

"Let's order room service, okay? But guys, can we all stay in this room tonight? I'm a bit freaked out," said Emily, dark eyes glistening from beneath a high forehead, her dark hair pulled back behind her. Coach called her "the sweet one." Her grandparents had been forced into the Japanese internment camp in Pinedale, just north of Fresno, during the second World War, and she said they had told her stories of that time to help her stay strong.

Now definitely seemed like a good time to be strong.

It also seemed like a good time for that room service.

"Yeah, of course," Jake said.

We were too nervous to eat much of anything we ordered from the hotel kitchen. Mostly we just watched the TV for updates. There weren't many. We girls eventually fell asleep on the beds, while the guys bunked on the floor. We all dozed restlessly. A few hours later, Turner unlocked the room and let himself in.

Conner raised his head sleepily, "Coach." He wiped his eyes. "What happened? Did you hear anything more?"

"No, Conner. I didn't get much more news, but I was able to rent a van and get money and some food. The van is all ready. I think we should head on out now, before the morning rush." Turner began rousing the other kids. "Wake up, everyone. Get packed. We're heading out as soon as possible."

"Are we going to take turns driving, Coach?" Caitlin asked as she pulled her shoes on.

"Eventually, yes. But I'm going to want to get at least 6-8 hours in myself in the beginning. You'll all have a chance to sleep the rest of the night," Turner said. "Hey, I want all the pillows and blankets from our rooms packed up too. We are in survival mode, people."

"Gotcha, Coach."

"Sure thing, Coach."

We all packed up quickly, and were down in the hotel parking garage and loading into the van when we heard a huge explosion.

"What the hell?" said DeAndre.

"Just get in! Hurry!" Turner hustled them all in and started up the big passenger van. He pulled out of the underground garage. It was nearing midnight and the streets were quiet. The few people on the street were all running toward a smoky area, likely where the blast had gone off.

"Perfect," Turner said, turning the other way. "Gives us a chance of getting out of this city."

Turner turned around and his determined eyes met our frightened faces. "Guys, just try and get comfy and sleep as much as you can. I am going to drive until sun-up, and then we can take turns. We should be able to make it home in 48 hours or so. It's about 3,000 miles. So: sleep now. Try to get some rest. Okay?"

"Coach, do you think our families are all right?" Conner asked.

"I don't know, Conner. Let's hope for the best and get there as fast as we can,"

"But what if the military won't let us get into town once we get closer?" I asked, "The news said the National Guard and the Marines had been called out to Palo Alto."

"We'll get as close as we can then," Turner replied, "We'll do as much as we can."

I sat back and looked around. The others were settling down with blankets and pillows. Staring out the window, I felt determined. There was no way anybody was going to stop us from getting back home. I needed to get to my family. As I watched the street lights go by, all I could think of was my grandparents, and my mom and my baby brother.

"Alyssa?" Emily whispered from the seat behind her, "I'm so scared."

"Don't worry," I replied, trying to sound stronger than I felt. "Let's just concentrate on getting as close to home as possible. Don't imagine more trouble than you have to."

Emily sniffed back unshed tears.

"Just try to get some sleep, okay?" I said, patting her arm.

"Okay." Emily sat back and closed her eyes, her head resting against the pillow.

I looked out the window again. The night was pitch black. We were just entering the Holland Tunnel. Soon we'd be in New Jersey. *Two miles down, 3,000 to go.* I thought.

Chapter Two

We drove all night and through the next two days, each of the four drivers taking turns. We made sure to keep the phones and iPad plugged in to the car chargers, so they'd always be ready. We eventually pulled into a Nevada gas station for a bathroom break, grabbing energy drinks and snacks as Coach filled up the tank. Coach Turner questioned the cashier while he paid for everything.

"Any word on the California situation?"

"Mack, they went black about three hours ago. Ain't no word - not a sound. I'm packin' up the missus' and we're heading east to her motha's in Iowa. No way we're stickin' around for this mess."

Turner grabbed the food and everyone bundled up in the van. He turned to us.

"Looks like everyone else is going in the opposite direction. But I still want to try and get as close as we can to home. No telling what we'll find in Fresno, but I can't stay away from my family and just leave them to whatever is going to happen. If some of you want to stay out of California, I understand."

"Coach Turner, I'm worried about my grandparents, mom and little brother," I said. "I want to get to them as fast as possible."

"Me, too," said Jacob. "Hey, I don't care what the authorities say. I want to get home now." The others agreed. Turner nodded.

"I just needed to make sure. We don't know what we're facing. It could be anything. It could be quite dangerous. Someone could get hurt," Turner said.

Everyone's faces remained resolute. The danger didn't matter, or at least we weren't thinking about it. We were determined. Tired and travel weary, we just wanted to get home. Every face looked worried.

But we were determined.

We all piled back into the van. I took a seat close to the back, and put my face against my bag and looked out the window. Exhaustion and worry battled for ownership of my head. My stomach churned with stress. I pulled out the almonds I had bought in the store, and took a swig of the RockStar energy drink in my lap and looked out the window. The stars twinkled in the clear night sky. Everything looked so peaceful. The heavens seemed oblivious to all the turbulence happening down here on Earth. What would we find when we pulled into town?

I dozed off within a half-hour and enjoyed three hours of sound sleep. That's what happens when you're exhausted. I woke up as the van slowed to a stop, lifting my head up for a look outside. We were stuck at a roadblock. Several police cars with flashing lights were parked in a V formation in the middle of the road, and officers were diverting all the traffic onto a side street.

Coach Turner stopped the van.

"Stay in your seats and sit tight, guys," he said, and then got out to see what he could find out from the cops.

"Where are we?" I asked Emily.

"We passed into California about two hours ago. We're near Barstow, maybe three miles out," said Conner, sitting across from her.

"The roadblock came up all of a sudden out of nowhere. There haven't been any other cars on the road with us until now," Emily said.

Everybody waited in silence; we were trying to hear what was being said outside. We could make out voices, but it was next to impossible to understand what they were discussing. After a tense ten minutes or so, Turner returned.

"They are turning back people to a detour, but I think we can still get farther in from here. They can't have enough cops out to block all the roads, and I know another way from here. It will just take a few extra hours," Turner said.

He turned the van to the left and started down a side road, then stopped about a half-mile down and pulled out a map book. After consulting it for a few minutes, he started up the van and continued down the road.

"Coach, need any help?" Jacob asked.

"No, I think I will take the rest of the way myself," Turner replied.

He followed the detour down to I-15, but then cut across the 395 and took some local roads. We were soon back on course, following frontage roads to Highway 58. I'd never seen so many trailer parks in my life. We crossed into some foothills near Tehachapi. More trailer parks, dusty-looking mountains and crops. Some Joshua trees here and there. Long stretches of road wound across what looked like a barren moonscape. It seemed unending, but I knew we were getting closer. I swallowed and looked nervously out the window again. The farther we drove, the more the knot in my stomach grew. I thought about my baby brother and my mom. Tanner was only 5 months old. I took out my wallet and looked at the photo I had of him, taken only last month.

"Who's that?" asked Caitlin.

"My baby brother, in Fresno," I answered.

"Very cute," she replied.

We both looked up as we heard Jacob talking to Coach Turner up front. They whispered, but we moved up closer, quietly, so we could hear better.

"… Jacob, I don't want to alarm the others. Don't ask me that," Turner said.

"Coach, my mom works in Palo Alto, I need to know. What are the updates coming out of the university?" Jacob asked.

Turner sighed. "Nothing good. Scattered reports of some kind of spreading death. The whole area has been cordoned off. The National Guard has been called in, the area involved is huge. They need to clear tens of thousands of people out of there. It's worse than the wildfires last year down south," he said.

"Do you know if the people who worked in the area got out? My mom works at Stanford. She's a history professor."

"I don't know, son." Turner said. The trouble apparently started at the university, in the biochemistry division. We should keep trying to get through on cell phones. Have you tried texting? Sometimes that gets through when phone signals won't."

Jacob sighed and got out his smartphone again. "I'll try texting now."

I suddenly remembered my iPad and got it out. I activated the hotspot on my smartphone and booted up the tablet.

Emily snored in her seat, but Caitlin leaned over and watched from behind.

"Can you get a signal?" she asked.

"I'm trying. The Evo takes a while to send to the iPad. Here, hmmm ..." I brought up Safari. It was slow to load; the mountains didn't allow much of a signal to get through. Then the window came up.

"I'm going to try CNN first," I said.

" 'K," Caitlin whispered, "God, I hope you can find some news."

It took me several tries to access the CNN website - it was probably close to crashing with so many people trying to get information. Finally I was rewarded by the familiar red banner.

"Coach!" I cried, "CNN has updates on Palo Alto," I walked up to the front to sit next to Turner.

"What does it say?" he asked.

I studied the website for several minutes. "It's going to take me awhile, but the latest news just says they are still trying to contain the infection. They haven't been successful. No word on whether the area was completely cleared out yet," I sat back to study the website more.

"Keep me posted on any updates. Refresh the site every few minutes if you can," Turner replied.

I settled back into my seat. The night grew longer, and the inky sky looked the same mile after mile as I kept refreshing the screen, hoping for something more.

"Hey," DeAndre whispered in my ear, "look on Twitter. The most up-to-date stuff is on Twitter."

I brought the website up.

"Try a few hashtags. Try #PaloAlto and #CaliforniaInfection," he suggested, looking over my shoulder.

I punched the keys and was rewarded.

"Oh, my God," Caitlin whispered next to me.

Twitter was wild with news. Devastating news. People were still trapped at the university. There was some kind of assault going on, police and something else. Family members were trying to reach the campus, but the roads had been closed. One person had gotten through on a dirt bike, only to be stopped by... something. His friends tweeted that he was down. It was hard to get a fix on exactly what was going on in Palo Alto. It was clear that the university had been under assault, and that the assault had spread to the city itself.

"What the hell's going on?" Conner asked. He crouched behind DeAndre and read along with us.

It wasn't clear at all, except that Palo Alto was a war zone. Tweets were coming fast and furious from users claiming to be at or near the university. They sounded desperate. It seemed like the infection had spread, but people weren't tweeting about sick people, they were tweeting about assaults. But by whom? The police? I typed in @PaloAltoPolice and started reading. It seemed like the police were nearly overwhelmed by the chaos, spread very thin, and barely keeping up with what was happening around them. Whatever it was, it was happening very fast, and it seemed to be spiraling out of control. When I refreshed, I saw a disturbing call for help to the Crescent Park area and beyond, past Gateway and reaching to the airport.

"This is spreading quickly," I said quietly.

"Check CNN again," said Caitlin. I clicked on the tab and refreshed the screen. "Oh, no."

A new story had loaded. They were evacuating a huge area. San Francisco was a little less than 35 miles from Palo Alto. They were evacuating San Francisco, San Jose, and as far south as Salinas. To the east, the police were asking for the area surrounding Modesto to evacuate. Fresno was about 165 miles away from Palo Alto, but I could see where this was going. The impacted circles were widening. At this rate, Fresno would be emptied within a day, maybe sooner.

"Coach," I said as I got up to approach the front of the van, "they're evacuating as far south as Salinas and all the way over to Modesto. I don't think it'll be long before it reaches Fresno. Whatever they're dealing with, it's moving fast. Real fast."

"God," he replied, rubbing his head. Then he remained quiet for a long minute. "I want to keep pushing forward; maybe we can get home before they clear out the city. We can get our families and evacuate out together," He said tiredly. "It should just be another two to three hours from here."

We nodded and went back to our seats. I had a very bad feeling about those assaults and went back to studying Twitter.

Caitlin and Emily huddled together and dozed off. Conner hunkered down with his phone, trying to get text messages out to his brother in Fresno. I pulled up my iPad again. The tweets coming out of the area sounded frantic and disjointed. Granted, 140 characters wasn't much. But these people sounded desperate and scared. I shivered.

"Want a blanket?" Jacob asked, offering me one. He had stopped trying to get text messages through to his mother. She wasn't responding. Neither was anybody else.

"Sure," I replied, "I'm cold, but I'm more worried. It makes the cold worse," I whispered as he wrapped the small blanket around my shoulders and settled in next to me.

"I don't know what we'll find, but I'm glad we're moving. Doing something. Not running away. That would drive me nuts," he said.

I nodded, and we settled back together to read Twitter. San Francisco was a mess. The whole county had well over 7 million residents, with over 805,000 people in the city proper itself. Plus, add to that the fact that it was waterlocked on three sides. Getting out of the city on a good day took an hour. With this emergency, it would be mass gridlock. I gulped. I hoped they would have enough time to get out before the infection hit the area. Why hadn't the police been able to contain this thing? I wondered. I needed to do more investigating. I wanted to know what we were up against. What would we be facing when we got into Fresno?

Twitter was both a blessing and a curse. Tweets from the front lines seemed to have tapered off, most of them coming during lulls in the assaults. But the attacks seemed nearly constant. And where were these assailants coming from? It's almost as if paratroopers were being dropped on the area from an unknown source. It was bizarre. And what was going on with the infection?

Then there were other tweets that seemed to be the work of practical jokers. Insane reports that couldn't possibly be true.

I settled back to wait, watching Coach drive onwards. He was determined to get to Fresno.

As morning neared and the sky began to brighten, we were finally making our way north through the valley. This giant depression in the middle of California had once been a vast inland sea, our geology teacher had told us. Now it was more like a desert. But it should have been humming with activity as residents took to the roads on their way to work.

It wasn't. The roads were nearly deserted, and police were moving quickly to seal off the area. We made it through Bakersfield, at the southern end of the valley, just in time. Police were setting up roadblocks, and we barely made it through. Now, we were approaching Selma, a small town about an hour and a half to the north.

"Shouldn't be long now, kids," Turner said over his shoulder, "maybe another half-hour."

I tried to call my mom again. No answer. 'All lines are busy' I sighed. My stomach was in knots. The waiting was driving me crazy. I turned my head to the window again, resting my cheek against the cool glass.

"Hey Alyssa, can I see your iPad for a minute?" Jacob asked next to me.

"Sure," I said, passing it to him, smiling. I had been reading Twitter for over an hour and my eyes were feeling the strain of focusing on the screen as the van bumped along. The road needed work in spots, and so did the shock absorbers.

"Thanks," he answered, gently taking the tablet from my hands and opening it back up. He began studying CNN and Twitter again. I settled back in my seat and stared out at the morning.

My dad had been gone for six months on deployment to Afghanistan. I missed him every day and found myself thinking how much I wished he were here with us now. I shivered again, drawing the blanket closer around my shoulders. I closed my eyes to rest and nodded off for a minute.

Opening my eyes again, I looked out the window. We had just gotten off the freeway and were and crossing over onto Ashlan Avenue. The streets were nearly deserted. Lights blazed in businesses, but it didn't look like anyone was inside the stores. Had the evacuation already occurred?

"I'm going to drop each of you off at your homes, okay? Then I'll go home myself," Coach Turner said to us over his shoulder, "Now, who lives where?"

"Coach, I live on Teilman Avenue," Emily said.

"I live on Thorne," said Caitlin.

"I'm on Arthur Avenue, Coach," said Conner.

"Alyssa and I both live on Feland, Coach," said Jacob.

"Coach, I'm right up here on the Fruit," piped DeAndre.

"Okay, that's closest I think, so let's hit DeAndre's house first," Turner said.

We all gathered up our suitcases, jackets and other belongings and moved toward the front. Turner pulled onto Fruit, following DeAndre's directions, and three minutes later we were stopped outside a green and white house with white roses growing along a picket fence.

"Come on, son. Let's see if anyone's home," Coach Turner said, leading DeAndre down from the van and across the sidewalk. They knocked on the door, and a young girl answered. It was his neighbor Risa, who had come to most of our plays. DeAndre's mom usually took her, and the little girl was a familiar sight, sitting there in the front row with a big smile on her face. Now, though, she looked scared.

"Your mom left early this morning and hasn't come back. It's just me here with Scooter," she said, as Scooter barked between her legs at the door. Even from our seats in the van, it wasn't hard to hear what the girl was saying. Her voice was elevated, and the slightest sound traveled across the dead air like a rock out of a slingshot.

"Risa is only 7, Coach. Mom watches her on the weekends. She wouldn't have left her alone this long normally," DeAndre said worriedly.

Coach thought for a moment. "Risa, get your things together, and come with us," he said. "DeAndre, I'm not comfortable leaving you here."

DeAndre nodded.

"Can Scooter come too?" asked Risa.

"Yes, but hurry, just grab some clothes and food. Here, we'll help," Turner replied.

They had food and clothes bundled in the van with Risa and Scooter within five minutes.

"My name is Alyssa, Risa. Come sit by me," I offered. She sat next to me and took my hand. Scooter lay down by her feet.

"OK, let's try the next house," Turner said, getting up into the driver's seat and starting up the van again.

"I think mine is next up, Coach, on Arthur," Conner said.

"Okay," Turner said. "Arthur is next then. Let's find out what's going on in this city."

As he drove up the street we looked out the windows. It was still early, and the houses looked empty. No one was getting ready for work, no one was outside getting the morning paper, no dogs barked, no kids lined up for school buses. The city looked deserted. It was very spooky. As we pulled up to Conner's block, Coach turned and said, "Everyone stay in here and wait for me. Conner, just let me see what's going on, okay?"

"Okay, Coach," we all answered in scared voices.

We pulled up to the curb and Coach Turner turned engine off and got out of the van. Stepping onto the grass outside the yellow house, he stopped and listened. The neighborhood seemed to hold its breath. We all watched from the windows of the van. Turner quietly walked up to the front door and knocked. Then he rang the doorbell and waited. From the van, we thought we could hear faint sounds coming from inside the house. It was hard to tell if it was just an animal or a person, but it seemed to be in some kind of distress. Turner grabbed the doorknob and turned it…

Screams filled the morning air, coming from inside the house. Coach swung open the door, ready for anything. Meanwhile, in the van, we had heard the screaming and we all began pouring out of the vehicle, scrambling to catch up with him. I wanted Risa and the dog to stay behind. I wanted them safely in the back of the van.

"Stay right here, Risa! Do not open the door of this van." I told her. Risa just looked at me with scared eyes. I tried again. "Do you understand me? Keep the door closed! Stay inside! Okay?" This time she nodded. Her dog lay under the seat, and she sat on the floor and put her arm around him. I jumped out of the van and shut the door firmly. Conner was in the lead as we ran up to the front door and came to a stop in our mad rush. We peered inside. Coach Turner was right in front of us.

Turner slowly stepped into the house. The screaming had stopped for a few seconds. Suddenly, it started up again, sounding panicked.

"That is my mom!" screamed Conner, and he rushed inside and came to a halt next to Turner.

They both rushed forward and around the right hand corner of the hall. They were in the kitchen, but the screams now came from directly ahead and to the left, in the family room. They both saw the scene at the same time, and Conner gasped in horror. His mother appeared to have fallen across the coffee table and onto the couch. Crouched over her was Conner's big brother Russell. He wasn't supposed to be there. He was supposed to be away at school.

At Stanford.

He wasn't. Instead, he was bent over his mother, his mouth

fastened to her flesh at the place where her neck met her shoulder. She screamed again as he bit down harder. Blood rushed out from around his mouth, and he let out a low groan that sounded surprisingly loud.

"Holy …!" exclaimed Coach Turner, looking around for some kind of weapon. Conner reached out and grabbed his big brother by the arm, "Get off mom!" he screamed. Russell growled and swung toward Conner, and we could all see his face. It was greyish black. Emily screamed involuntarily. Russell stood there, one hand holding his mother, and one foot turned toward us, indecisive. He let out a low growl. Turner took that moment to swing a chair at him that he'd grabbed from the kitchen. It hit him solidly in the head and chest, and he fell to the ground. Turner jumped on Russell and held the chair against him, pinning him to the floor as the crazed man bucked and screamed incoherently.

"Grab your mother, Conner!" Turner yelled as he tried to stay on top of Russell.

Conner and Jacob grabbed the dazed and bloodied woman and dragged her through the kitchen and out the door onto the lawn, where she lay on the grass. They then set to the task of staunching her bleeding wounds with some towels they'd grabbed on their way out.

Turner, meanwhile, was losing the fight. Russell's face and hands were discolored, his clothes were torn and he had scratches all over him. I sniffed the air and smelled something, I wasn't sure what, but it wasn't good. Russell roared and pushed at the chair on his chest. He got his head and shoulders up off the ground where he had been pinned a moment earlier.

"Get into the van! I can't hold him much longer! Get Conner's mother into the van!" yelled Turner.

I scrambled over to help him push against Russell, both of us leaning our weight onto the chair across his torso, and he fell back down to the ground again. DeAndre and Caitlin ran outside and relayed Coach's message. I heard them dragging Conner's mom across the lawn and into the van. She screamed with every jarred movement. Risa's dog started barking. Then DeAndre rushed back in, "okay, she's in."

"Let's go together, Alyssa. On the count of three. One. Two. Three!" Coach said.

We both gave Russell one last push, then ran like crazy for the front door. Slamming it behind us, we sprinted for the van. I scrambled in as Coach Turner ran around to the driver's side and jumped in. He put the key in the ignition and started the engine. I slammed my door just as the house door flew open and Russell staggered out, making noises that sounded like deep-throated growls. His face was a greyish black color that seemed to darken as he staggered across the lawn, toward us. As Turner threw the van into gear and peeled away from the curb, the thing that had been Russell made one last grab at us. He reached for us, his hand grazing the rear bumper as we pulled away and he fell into the gutter. Turner watched him in the rearview mirror as he sped down the street.

"Man, what the hell was with that guy?" exclaimed Jacob.

Conner just shuddered and held his mother. His face was white with shock.

"I can't believe this is happening," Turner said, turning a corner. Up ahead was a minimart. "We need to tell somebody about what just happened, warn the authorities," he said, turning into the store's driveway and parking the van.

Coach looked out tentatively. There was movement inside, but the parking lot was nearly deserted, something I'd never seen before. This convenience store was usually a hive of activity, day or night. Turner honked a few times, and waited. Then he sat up straighter as two men came running out the doors.

"Thank goodness," Turner said, then he looked closer. The men were running, but they looked odd, as if they were lurching as they ran, and they seemed directionless, weaving to and fro as they made their way across the pavement to the waiting van. Turner froze. The men's faces were both dark grey.

"Oh my God," said Turner. "Do NOT open the doors."

The two men had arrived at the van. They didn't seem to realize where the door was. One of them came up against the front windshield, and his blackened hands scrambled against the glass as his mouth opened to emit a low groan. The palms of his hands were scratched and bloody. The other man banged up behind the first, then came around the left side of the van to look through the windows. Both had blackened, discolored faces and were barefoot. Their eyes didn't seem to focus correctly and seemed almost glazed over with a white film.

"Jesus," Jacob exclaimed, "They're the same!"

Risa began to cry quietly. I just put my arm around her and held her close. I stared out the window at the two men in amazement.

Turner quickly put the van in reverse and backed away from them. They stumbled after us, looking almost drunk. Turner grimly turned the van around and drove away.

In the back, Conner's mother gave out a moan. She sounded like she was in a great deal of pain.

"We've got to go somewhere safe where we can get her medical attention," Coach said, "I'm going to try a hospital. I'm going to try Saint Agnes. I hope they're open and working."

"What the heck is going on?" DeAndre exclaimed. "It's like the whole city's gone mad!"

"I think it has to do with the virus, D," I said quietly. DeAndre looked at me. "Apparently it traveled faster than we'd hoped," I whispered, shaken.

Conner held his mother to him and quietly began praying, "Hail Mary, full of grace..."

"That's not a bad idea," Turner said grimly. "Something tells me we're going to need all the help we can get."

He drove silently through the city as the sun rose higher in the sky. Herndon Avenue, the main expressway running west to east at the north end of the city, was nearly deserted. We saw a few people off in the distance, but there was no way to tell whether they were affected. After what seemed like a long time, but was in reality just about 10 or 15 minutes, we arrived at Saint Agnes Medical Center.

Chapter Three

"Mom?" Conner said in a quavering voice, "Mom?"

I approached him and his mother, "What's her name, Conner?" I asked quietly.

"Her name is Debby. She's only 38 years old," Conner whispered, fighting back tears. "Do you think she'll be okay?"

"I don't know," I answered honestly. I took ahold of Debby's hand gently. Then I focused on her face. "Debby?" I said gently, "can you hear me?"

Her lips moved, but at first nothing came out. Then: "y-y-yes."

"We're taking you to a hospital. Just stay still. You're going to be okay," I said. Then I checked her shoulder wound, lifting the towels that were pressed against it. It seemed to have stopped bleeding, but the bite was ragged. It looks like Russell had been at his mom for a while. Her face was bloody, her cheek and lip torn and bleeding. I stayed next to Conner, holding Debby's hand. The van soon pulled up to the emergency entrance of Saint Agnes Medical Center. As Turner pulled up to the Emergency Room, several ambulances were there as well. We could see medical personnel milling about the area. They looked fine.

"Oh, thank God!" Turner exclaimed.

We all got out and helped Conner carry Debby into the ER. Risa left her dog in the van and followed us inside. I took her hand and smiled down at her, trying to reassure her. Conner and Coach Turner remained with Debby and talked to the nurses. The rest of us milled about, looking around. I headed off to find a bathroom. DeAndre, Jacob and Emily walked up to some vending machines. Caitlin and Risa followed me.

"I can't believe this is happening," Caitlin mumbled, she was shivering as we walked into the women's bathroom. I headed straight to the washbasin. I was filthy after the ordeal at Conner's house. I began washing my hands with warm soap and water.

"Yea," I whispered, "God…" I leaned for a minute against the sink with my eyes closed. I felt exhausted. None of us had gotten much sleep since we'd left New York on our two-day ordeal in the van.

I washed my face next, and my arms, trying to get clean again. Something about that Russell guy just made me feel gross and unclean. I scrubbed my arms so hard they turned pink. Caitlin beside me was doing the same, sobbing quietly. Finally, after many minutes, I felt clean enough to stop. I turned and went into a stall.

"Risa, try to clean up your hands and face, okay honey?" I said. Risa slowly began to wash her hands.

"I hope we can change our clothes soon, I feel so dirty after that drive and what happened at Conner's," said Caitlin.

"Me too," I answered, finishing up and exiting the stall. Caitlin was just entering one. I decided to stay until she was finished so we could leave together. I sighed and closed my eyes as I leaned up against the sink counter. I felt exhausted. I heard Caitlin finish up.

"Come on, let's go find the guys," I said.

We went out and looked around. Coach Turner and Emily were there.

"The others are in the bathroom," he said, and then turned to Emily, "Em, you should go wash up, 'k?"

I decided to walk around and stretch my feet as Emily went to wash up. I walked down the corridor and then up again, keeping the others in sight. The boys joined us a few minutes later, and a little while later, Emily was there, too.

"Any word on Debby, Coach?" I asked.

"They're working on her now. The problem isn't the bite so much as the possible infection. The doc said the hospital is already over capacity, I'm not sure if they'll be able to keep her here," he said wearily.

He went to sit down, then changed his mind and headed to the bathroom to wash up. He looked pretty grungy. Wrestling with Russell had messed him up a bit. We all sat down in some chairs nearby. As we settled in, a wild-eyed woman ran into the Emergency Room, holding a small child.

"Help me! Somebody help! My son!" she cried.

Two nurses ran up to her and took the child from her arms. He looked to be no more than 4. It was hard to see, but he looked bloody and unconscious. His mother followed the nurses as they raced down the hall with the little body. I couldn't tell if he was breathing or not. I shuddered. Fresno was turning into a very scary place. Almost like a war zone.

"My God," exclaimed Jacob quietly. Just then Emily came out of the bathroom and joined us.

"What happened?" she asked.

"This lady just came in with her little boy, he looked like he was hurt bad, he was totally limp," DeAndre said.

Emily stood there, holding her arms and looking down the corridor. We could still hear the mom crying. Then a door shut and the ER went quiet again, except for a voice on the intercom calling out for different medical personnel. We sat for a while, then I got up to go look at the vending machines.

"Anything good over there?" I asked as I walked away holding Risa's hand.

"They've got energy drinks and candy bars, mostly," DeAndre said, getting up to walk with me. "I couldn't eat anything. This whole mess has made me so queasy," he finished.

I scanned the three machines that were there. Nothing looked good to me. I got a couple of Monster energy drinks for later and tucked them into my pockets. I bought Risa a candy bar and an apple juice. For myself, I considered the candy bars, then went for a bag of chips. Munching on them, we walked back to the chairs with DeAndre in tow. Wearily I sat down again. The chips were tasteless. I sighed and closed my eyes, leaning my head back. Risa sat next to me and rested against me, exhausted. Jacob came to sit next to me on my other side, and took my hand in his. I opened my eyes and smiled at him gratefully. He smiled back. I leaned my head on his shoulder and closed my eyes again. All of a sudden I felt exhausted. My eyes opened again as Conner came up to us.

"Conner, what's going on?" DeAndre asked.

"The doctors got the bleeding stopped and stitched her up. But they said she was probably infected. The wound on her neck was already turning a funny color, Coach," He turned to Turner, "I don't know what's going to happen. Can you go talk to them? They wouldn't tell me much."

“Sure, son,” Turner said, and walked away to talk to the doctors.

“Conner,” Jacob said, “Is your mom gonna stay here?”

“I’m not sure. I think so,” Conner answered. He sat down wearily.

“I’m gonna hit the bathroom. Be back in a minute, guys,” Jacob said.

“Want a Coke?” I asked Conner. He nodded and I got up and went to the machines. Risa tagged along, slipping her hand into mine.

“Alyssa, I’m scared,” Risa said to me after a minute.

“I know, honey. Me too,” I said. I picked out a Vanilla Coke and a bag of Doritos for Conner and we headed back. I was exhausted. After I gave him the snacks, I settled back in my seat with Risa, and we both closed our eyes. I felt as if I could fall asleep right there in that chair. Every muscle hurt. I hadn’t had a full night’s sleep for days.

I hadn’t nodded off for five minutes when a scream pierced the air in the Emergency Room. I opened my eyes to chaos. From the corridor where Coach Turner had disappeared came several frantic screams. I jumped up and grabbed Risa’s hand and, without thinking, I sprinted down that corridor. The others ran after me, they had jumped at the sounds too.

Our tennis shoes squeaked in the polished hallway as I led the small group of us down the hall at a run. This was no longer the safe haven I had first taken it for. I wanted to get Coach and get the heck out of there fast. Something was happening, and I had felt it for a while. I hadn’t realized what the feeling was until now, but for the last half-hour I had felt a strange, unsettled lump in the pit of my stomach.

We ran down the curving corridor, and I nearly ran head on into

Coach Turner. He was crouched in the middle of the hallway, screaming, with Debby in a hospital gown bent over him. As I came to a sudden stop, trying not to fall over them, I saw that she was biting down on his neck and shoulder. She heard me and looked up. Her dark brown face was beginning to turn a strange opaque black and her mouth was full of dripping blood, a piece of Turner's neck hanging from her teeth. Turner seemed woozy from pain and stumbled to the side. Debby grabbed him again even as she began to chew and swallow the flesh in her mouth.

"Mom!" cried Conner.

"Ahhh!" I screamed at the same time, and without thinking, I kicked her away from Coach and grabbed his arm. He was dazed and bleeding profusely from his head, but he got up and ran with me. We all started back the way we had come.

"Run! Go, now! Come on!" I yelled, barely pausing as I ran back the way we had come. I glanced down the hallway as I ran. Debby and five others people were walking down the corridor toward us. When I say walking, it was more like a stumbled lurching. Blood coated their mouths and the bottom halves of their faces. The skin on all of them had a greyish-black tinge to it. Their legs didn't seem to work as well as they should. Their arms swung in a funny way, too. But their eyes: there wasn't a darned thing funny about their eyes. Although their eyes seemed to be turning somewhat opaque, they were fixed on us. Our pursuers emitted low groaning sounds as they stumbled forward, and their eyes never wavered from their prey. That was what freaked me out: they looked at us with hungry looks. Their eyes never blinked. Their grey faces were blank except for those eyes. So much expression in those eyes.

I made a strangled sound and turned again to run in the direction I had just come from. Risa had seen those people too, and she almost outpaced me. But then the unthinkable happened. As we ran all out, Risa stumbled after me, trying to keep up. I hung on to her hand, but

I was going too fast for her, and she fell. She hit the corridor floor hard and her head made a ringing thud as it hit the floor. I grabbed her and tried to get her up, but her eyes were closed and her head bled at the crown. She was nearly unconscious and there was no time to stop, so I grabbed her and flung her over my shoulder and kept running. Conner and Emily helped Coach Turner run and we began again to make our way down the corridor. Those people were right behind us, but we ran hard and drew away from them.

The lot of us ran down the hall, stopping only to grab our stuff from the chairs before running out of the doors we had entered not an hour previously.

"Come on, guys!" I screamed, handing Risa to DeAndre and fumbling in Coach's pockets for the van keys. We heard new screams coming from the waiting room. Those grey lurching people had come into the room and as I looked through the glass doors I saw one grey man with a bloody face grab a woman who had been sitting near us. He held her and bit down on her face. She screamed as blood poured from the bite. He continued gnawing on her and, paralyzed with fear, she seemed incapable of anything but screaming as he destroyed the left side of her face. I turned and helped get Risa and Turner into the van, then scrambled into the driver's seat.

"Are we all in?" I yelled as I started the van.

"Jacob was in the bathroom! He's still in there! Oh My God!" screamed Emily. As she said this, Jacob sprinted out the doors at top speed. He was on the track team as well as the theatre club, and he flew like the wind.

It's a good thing Jacob ran so fast, because Conner's mom was in hot pursuit. Conner opened the door and waved to Jacob, who sprinted toward us. When he reached the van, he jumped in, slamming the doors with about 10 seconds to spare. Debby was right behind him, and as I threw the van into reverse, she lurched up to the vehicle, slapping the driver's-side window with a bloody hand.

"MOM!!!" sobbed Conner.

"OH SHIT!" I exclaimed as I squealed the tires and drove in reverse away from the nightmare that had been Conner's mother only an hour ago. In a move that would make any NASCAR driver proud, I sped backwards and then wrenched the wheel and flipped the van forward, slamming the gearshift into drive and gunning the engine, so that we peeled out of the parking lot on two wheels. We must have been doing 50 mph. There was a minute there when we almost tipped to the left, but I got the van under control and sped down the road, leaving the nightmare behind us.

Chapter Four

We all sat in stunned silence as we sped away from the area and onto the freeway. I was putting as much distance between us and the area as I could, as fast as I could. No one could blame me: any one of them would have done the same thing had they been driving. Probably would have flipped the van going around that corner, too. After a few minutes, I turned to the others.

"How is Coach doing? Is everybody else okay?" I asked quietly, "anybody else hurt? Anyone else get touched by those freaks?"

I looked back momentarily and saw Jacob and Caitlin trying to staunch Coach's bleeding. He looked unconscious. They wrapped his head tightly with a t-shirt.

Everyone else was okay. Nobody else had been hurt, and no one else had been touched. Coach looked bad, but I turned back and concentrated on driving. I wanted to put as much distance between us and that hellhole as possible.

Conner sat looking out the window, silent tears running down his face. Leaving his mom behind probably hadn't been as shocking as seeing how crazy she had become. How crazy all those nuts had become. Conner wasn't alone. Everyone had a shell-shocked look, me included, I guessed. But I also felt a determination. I looked out the window, and the breeze felt welcoming and cool. I sighed and drove on, looking all around. I glanced in the rearview mirror, half-consciously afraid that those people – those creatures – might somehow be following us. I wanted to know what was around me at all times: I had to know if anything else crazy was going to happen. I felt jumpy. The last three days had been nuts.

And now there were so many questions. Where should we go now? And what the hell were those people about? The way their skin looked, like it was turning greyish-black, the way they lurched when they walked, as if their legs didn't quite work right, was absolutely freaky. And especially the way they attacked people and tried to friggin' eat them. My God. I shuddered. They were acting like every cliché of zombies I had ever seen in the movies. But that couldn't be. Could it? I took a deep breath and made a silent wish. I wanted to know everything that had caused this to happen, I wanted to know why Conner's mom had changed. And I thought of something else.

"Guys? Keep a good eye on Coach Turner and let me know if he comes to again, okay? I don't know exactly what we're up against, but I don't want him doing what Debby did after she was injured. Jacob, about how long did it take from when Russell attacked Debby to when we brought her to the hospital?" I asked.

"Jesus, Alyssa, I don't think it was more than an hour or so," Jacob said, looking worried.

We needed to get Coach somewhere fast, somewhere other than the van. We needed to be safe.

As I drove, I thought quickly. The people at the hospital had looked wrong. Their faces had been greyish, and one looked to be turning almost black. They had almost looked like week-old corpses. I shuddered. The freeway was deserted. The sun was bright in the clear, deep blue sky. Looking out on the city from the freeway, I could see that the local streets were also deserted. I think I saw only one or two cars in ten minutes, and those seemed to be heading out of the area too. I just wanted to get to safety. This city felt haunted.

"How are Coach and Risa doing?" I asked over my shoulder.

Caitlin came forward to talk to me. "Risa is still unconscious," she said. "Coach is halfway awake but looks worse. I wrapped his wound, but it doesn't look good. And he feels like he's starting the run a fever. I'm worried. We need to get him some help soon."

"Okay, let me know if his fever gets really high. I'm going to try to get to the Bakersfield hospital, but I'm not sure if driving for two hours with a dangerous fever would be the best thing for Coach," I said.

Caitlyn patted my shoulder and turned to make her way back to Coach.

I tried to see past everyone's heads to the back of the long van. Coach Turner was settled against the corner of the seat in the back. He was moaning softly and he had begun to thrash against the sides of the van.

"His fever is worse, Alyssa. He looks bad. I think we should try to bring his temperature down. He's burning up," Conner said.

I slowed the van and pulled it off to the side of the freeway, looking around nervously. Everything looked clear. I went back to check on them myself. I bent over Coach and got a good look at him. I was worried I would find him turning grey, like Debby had done before she went nuts. But he wasn't grey at all, he was bright pink. His face was flushed and sweaty, and he had twin white spots on either cheek. He was unconscious and groaning softly in his sleep. His head moved back and forth like he was having a nightmare. He groaned louder in his sleep. I put a hand under his jaw, taking his temperature the way my grandmother had taught me to do when you didn't have a thermometer. He felt so hot to my touch. In fact, his face burned my palm. I drew back.

"Oh, Coach," I whispered.

We had all had a year's worth of acting classes with Coach Turner. We'd performed a dozen skits and plays under his direction. His infectious laughter and passion for acting were constants in our lives. To see him like this, when he had done so much to bring us safely home, brought a lump to my throat.

I was astonished at how hot he had gotten in the last half-hour. At this rate, he wouldn't make it to a hospital - he wouldn't even last another hour. I thought about the possibility of us all staying at my house for the day, until we could bring Coach's fever down. Maybe we could send for help. I wondered if 911 was still working. Looking down at Coach again, I made a decision.

"I don't think he will last if we keep going. We owe him so much, we owe it to him to try and help him." I thought for a moment. We were about ten minutes from my house, and I didn't feel safe taking us somewhere unknown, not after what had happened at the hospital. I looked up into their faces.

"I'm taking us to my house. It's close by and we can get him into a bed and try to help him there. I think if we were to try to make it to Bakersfield, Coach won't make it, not with a fever this high."

Everyone nodded.

I looked over at Risa.

"How's she doing?" I asked, feeling her temperature. It was normal. Her head was wrapped in a t-shirt, and they had cleaned most of the blood off her face. I hoped she would be okay.

I looked back at the others. They were all worried and scared. Putting on a strong face, I slid back into the driver's seat and started the van again. As I pulled back onto the freeway and headed toward home, my heart felt heavy with a growing sense of hopelessness. I had a very bad feeling about this.

Driving onward down the freeway toward home, I swallowed. I didn't know what to expect. I hoped I wouldn't find more of those weird people. My nerves were taut and my head hummed. I felt alert. But that was okay, I wanted to be this awake if I came across those people again. I had to be able to react. I cracked open the icy Red Bull Jacob had handed me and took a long swig. The fizzy energy drink hit my throat with a welcomed burn, and I took another long drink. It tasted so good.

Five minutes later I pulled up to the curb outside my house. Stopping the engine, I looked around the neighborhood. The area looked deserted. I unbuckled my seatbelt and turned to the others.

"Jacob, Conner, DeAndre; try and get him inside. Put him in the back bedroom. Everyone, let's get into the house, maybe stay until nightfall. We've got to try and get his fever down to something he can survive, or he'll never make it to the hospital in Bakersfield. Okay, let's go," I said. Scooter followed me into the house. A quick search of the property showed that it was deserted. I put Scooter into the backyard and went back to the van. As everyone settled in the house, I pulled the van into our empty garage.

"Well, at least Mom and the baby got out in the evacuation," I said under my breath as I pulled the parking brake and shut the engine off. I got out and pressed the garage door button to close the large, heavy barrier. Seeing my mom's car gone from its usual parking place in here had left me with mixed emotions. I was glad they had gotten out of the city, and yet the sight of the big, cavernous garage completely empty had made me feel so completely alone in the world I felt like crying. Locking the van, I pocketed the keys in my jeans pocket and wrapped my arms around my elbows, shivering. After a moment I quickly entered the house through the inner garage door, shutting the light off and locking the door after me. Walking through the kitchen to join the others, I quietly berated myself. This was no time for those kinds of feelings.

Jacob and DeAndre had settled Coach in the back bedroom.

"Do you think we should restrain him, guys? Remember Debby," I said looking down at Coach's sleeping form.

"We just wanted to get him settled in, Alyssa," Jacob said. "He's still unconscious and hotter than ever."

"I'll get some aspirin and the ice packs. And a thermometer. I want to know exactly how high his fever is," I said, feeling his neck and forehead again. "He feels so hot it's burning my hand. Maybe I'm cold. It can't be that high…" I went to hunt for a thermometer.

As I made my way back toward the kitchen, Emily stopped me in the hall.

"Risa is tucked into the spare bed, Alyssa. She's still unconscious, but her temperature and breathing are fine," she said, stretching.

"Okay, that sounds good. Hopefully she'll come to soon. Meanwhile, get some food for yourself and try to rest, okay?" I said.

She nodded, patting me on the shoulder, and followed me down the hall and into the kitchen where Conner and Caitlyn were already eating.

"How're you guys holding up?" I asked as I passed them.

Conner had his face buried in a huge bowl of Cap'n Crunch cereal, and just glanced up and mumbled incoherently. I smiled tiredly. Caitlyn was wolfing down a couple of hot dogs she had microwaved.

"I feel tons better now that I'm eating," she said between bites. "This hot dog tastes like heaven."

I went past them and into the garage, where my mother kept

some spare medical supplies. I found a thermometer and some aspirin, and made my way back inside, locking the door behind me. I felt a little paranoid doing this in my own house, but things weren't the same at all. On the way back through the kitchen, I grabbed six ice packs out of the freezer. Conner finished the last of his cereal and followed me, carrying four more. We hurried back to the rear bedroom and packed them under Coach's shirt. He moaned in his sleep and then settled down. I held the thermometer up to Coach Turner's ear. The reading was 108. That couldn't be right. I blinked and shook my head and cleared it again and snapped a new plastic cover on it and inserted it again. 108. Stunned, I looked at Coach's face. He was definitely still alive, but at that temperature, he would soon have brain damage.

"We've got to get him into the bathtub, the ice packs aren't going to drop his fever fast enough," Jacob said next to me. I nodded, and we all proceeded to strip Coach to his t-shirt and boxers, and wrestle him into the bathtub. I turned the water on and adjusted it to a tepid temperature. As it filled, Coach moaned and struggled weakly, trying to climb out of the tub, even though his eyes were still closed.

"The water feels freezing to him in his state, we may have to hold him down," I said.

Conner leaned over Coach's head and held his shoulders down. DeAndre, Jacob and I held his torso and legs. Coach Turner began thrashing harder as the water filled the tub. We were all getting soaked. As the tub filled up, I kneeled down to get a better grip on his legs. We held him in the water for 15 minutes; it was exhausting work. Finally, I took his temperature again and it was 101.

"That's pretty good. Let's get him back in bed guys," I said.

Soaked and exhausted, we toweled him off and got him settled in bed. He moaned in his sleep, still unconscious. His temperature had gone way down, but his color didn't look good. Instead of red and flushed, his face was turning pale. I pulled a blanket over him and then checked his eyes. They seemed dilated, and the rims were turning bright red. He was so sick.

"Oh, Coach," I whispered. I got up and looked at the others gathered in the room.

"I'll sit with him first, Alyssa. Then maybe we can switch in a couple of hours," Conner said.

"Do you think we should restrain him or something?" DeAndre asked.

"Well, he's asleep now," Conner said.

"D's right, Conner. I'm going to go find something to tie him up with," I said. "Be back in a minute. I stepped into the hallway and checked the closet. There were some scarves, which I grabbed.

"Here, these will hold him, they're silk and very strong," I said, handing them to Jacob and Conner to tie Coach up with. They made quick work of the job, and soon Conner was sitting in the chair next to the bed, with Coach tied down. I nodded.

We made our way down the hall and into the kitchen. I grabbed a banana, peeled it and began to eat it. Jacob put a couple of hot dogs in the microwave. DeAndre and Caitlyn made themselves bowls of cereal. We all ate in silence. After I finished my banana, I started in on an apple. As my teeth crunched into the juicy fruit, I began to relax a little. Munching on the apple, I walked out of the kitchen and headed to the front of the house. After checking to be sure the locks were all secure and the windows shut, I made my way to the rear patio.

Opening the sliding glass door, I stepped out into the midday sunshine and looked around the large yard. The air was warm and muggy and the sky was still a clear, deep blue. I stopped chewing my apple for a minute and listened to the neighborhood. It was still utterly quiet. Scooter was asleep on one of the patio chairs. Not a dog barked, not a bird chirped, no people, cars or motorcycles could be heard. It sounded like a tomb. I was thoroughly creeped out. Opening the door again, I stepped inside. As I crossed back to the kitchen, finishing my apple and throwing it into the trash, my stomach began to feel queasy.

"I'm going to go check on Coach and Conner," I said to the others. But before I could make two steps down the hallway, we all heard a yelp coming from the back bedroom. It was Conner's voice. Another, louder cry issued forth, but was cut off abruptly. Jacob, DeAndre and I sprinted to the bedroom. I was the first to round the corner and enter the doorway, and the sight that greeted my eyes made me cry out in horror.

Chapter Five

Two of the walls of the room were heavily sprayed with blood, dripping down to the rug. Coach was crouched on the far side of the room, behind the bed. The scarves hung from his arms, torn and bloody. Conner was nowhere to be seen. Jacob gasped behind me, moved around me to see what Turner was doing, and then let out another gasp. Growls and slurps could be heard, and a thumping sound. I edged further in, to peer at what Jacob was seeing.

"Oh my God…" I said. Coach was on all fours, crouched over Conner. Conner's leg was weakly pumping up and down, and as we watched, it slowed to a stop. Coach had ripped his throat out, and was focused on chewing at Conner's neck like a dog. We could see Conner's face, eyes wide open but unseeing. As his kicking leg fell still, and all we could hear was the sound of Coach Turner eating at Conner's lifeless body. It had all happened in the space of a few minutes. We could hear the sound of Caitlyn and Emily coming down the hall and into the room behind us. Caitlyn gasped and cried out, and Emily started screaming, "Coach!" This caught the attention of the thing that used to be our teacher, and he swung his head around to the noise. We all gasped as one, because Coach Turner's face was covered in Conner's blood, and what skin we could see was turning dark grey. He focused his eyes on us, bared his teeth and made a low, menacing growl.

Jacob turned quickly and said, "Get out, everyone! OUT!" as he scrambled for the door himself. We all backed up hurriedly into the hallway, and Jacob shut and locked the door as the zombie that had been Coach Turner threw himself against the thin wood. A two-foot crack appeared in the middle of the door, and we all ran.

"Get to the van, everyone! That door won't hold for long!" I cried as I dashed through the kitchen and into the garage, fumbling for only a second at the locked garage door. Another crash was heard as Coach tried to get through the door. It sounded insane. Jacob stopped and crept back towards the hallway, and I whispered, "What are you doing?"

Jacob held a finger to his lips and pointed to the near bedroom where Risa still slept. In our panic we had almost left without her. My heart beat faster. I paused behind him, and with DeAndre, we crept back toward the hallway. The back bedroom door was still. Maybe Coach had stopped trying to get through the door and had turned his attention back to Conner's body. I felt my eyes tear up as I thought of Conner. Jacob quietly walked back into the hallway and into the front bedroom to gather Risa up. As I watched from the doorway, he lifted the sleeping girl and turned toward me. He was steady and strong holding Risa, but as I looked into his eyes I saw unshed tears. He blinked them away and came forward, and I backed up out of his way. I turned my head and listened again for noise from the closed door at the end of the hall. There was a faint scraping sound and fumbling. What was that thing doing in there? I wondered.

I thought for a moment, then turned into my mother's bedroom behind me. She was a fanatic for everything Japanese and there were a set of katanas – curved samurai swords - on a stand on her dresser. I grabbed the larger one and motioned for DeAndre to grab the smaller one of the pair. He nodded and we made our way back to the kitchen, right behind Jacob, who was holding Risa to his chest. As we passed through the kitchen door to the garage I locked it behind me.

I didn't know if zombies were smart enough to unlock a door, but I was hoping they weren't. Someone had moved the dog into the garage and he was already in the van. As Jacob, Risa, and DeAndre got in, I hit the garage door opener button, and the sound of the big door lifting was so loud I hoped the zombie that had been Coach Turner wouldn't come for us then. I put the key in the ignition and backed the van out of my garage. Emily and Caitlyn were crying softly. I felt a heaviness in my chest and felt my throat catch. I couldn't speak. I knew if I tried I would break into sobs. My face set, I backed the van onto the street and began to move forward as tears I could no longer contain fell down my face. We were all filled with shock and despair as I drove away from what we had thought would be a place of refuge. I took one more look at my home. It looked normal. Like nothing was wrong at all. Like my mom should come walking out into the yard any minute now, smiling and waving. I took a deep, shuddering breath and I felt fresh tears stream down my face. My God. I still couldn't believe what my eyes had seen. Coach Turner had morphed into a crazed zombie lunatic and had attacked and killed Conner. Conner! My God. My God. I slowed the van to a stop as my eyes closed in anguish, sobs threatening to overwhelm me. I could hear Caitlyn and Emily crying softly behind me. Conner had been such a good friend, and he had been my partner in two productions last year. I remembered how he had helped take care of Coach Turner for the past half day. I remembered how his mother had succumbed to the same sickness that had changed Coach. Now Conner was dead like his mother. What had happened to his father? I shook my head against the craziness of the world and how everything was getting more apocalyptic as the days wore on.

I blinked my eyes clear and took several deep breaths to steady myself. I had to remain strong. We had to get to safety. I began moving the van forward once more, looking from right to left as I drove. The neighborhood seemed deserted. All the families on my street had disappeared from their homes. Where were they? Where had they gone? There had been no note in my house at all, no sign where my mom and brother had evacuated to. Driving away from the neighborhood I had grown up in, I looked around some more. As I turned the corner toward the freeway, I thought I saw a blur out of the corner of my eye. I turned my head, but it was gone. Blinking my eyes, I proceeded through the neighborhood.

"See something?" Emily said, wiping her eyes as she came up to talk with me. She looked out through the front windshield.

"I don't know. I thought… well, it was a blur, could have been a dog or something," I said.

Emily shivered. She looked out the window again, scanning the area. She shook her head, stifling a sob.

"It's like the whole city is crazy! I don't know what to expect. I can't believe what just happened! My God, poor Conner." She began to cry again. "I'm worried about my parents, my brother … everyone I know," she whispered. "And where did everyone's families go? The houses all look deserted."

I patted her arm with one hand as I drove on with the other. I had the same questions going through my own head, the same sorrow for our friends. She wrapped her arms around herself, shivering. Although it wasn't cold, being this freaked out in our hometown, where everything should have been comfortable and normal, was very unsettling. I felt warmth in my chest for my friends. I wanted to find out what the heck was going on. I needed answers. I felt that if I kept moving us forward, we would find those answers, eventually.

Chapter Six

I wiped my eyes as I drove, trying to clear them. Jacob came up behind me and handed me a Kleenex, and I blew my nose several times.

"Hey, Alyssa, stop at my house, there's several things I want to get to defend ourselves, okay?" Jacob said quietly. I glanced at him. He was the oldest among us, having entered school a year later than the rest of us. His face was pale but his expression was set. He patted the katana beside me, and I understood. We needed defense.

"I'll go in with you, but I want the others to stay in the van," I said. Jacob nodded his agreement.

I drove the two blocks back to Jacob's house and pulled up to the curb.

"Emily, Caitlyn, DeAndre, stay here with Risa," I said, "we will be in and out fast."

The others agreed. I nodded my head. "Here're the keys, DeAndre. Be on the lookout. Lock the doors right after we leave, and keep watch. If you see anything crazy, honk the horn." I tossed him the keys, and then turned around again. We all looked out at the neighborhood. Everything looked still and quiet. "Okay, let's go as a unit and stay together," I instructed. Jacob was next to me. He nodded with a determined look on his face and gripped the seatback. "Let's go."

We left the van and jogged across the lawn. Jacob had his key out and quickly fitted it to the door lock. I paused, listening. "I don't hear anything," I said quietly. He turned the key, tense. Who knew what was behind that door? Our senses were alert for anything as it slowly opened.

The foyer looked empty. After a quick look around, we determined the house was empty. It looked like Jacob's family had left too. There was no note, nothing to tell where they had gone. I grabbed a trash bag and loaded it with food and blankets.

Jacob grabbed his father's rifle and shotgun and loaded up on ammunition.

"Just in case," he said. I nodded grimly. Food, blankets, pillows, extra coats and clothes. Jacob also grabbed a lockbox.

"My dad's emergency fund. Several thousand dollars," he explained.

"Sounds good to me. We'll need to get gas soon," I said. We were in and out in less than ten minutes. Back in the van, I blew air out of my mouth.

I got into the driver's seat, leaning forward to rest my forehead against the steering wheel and close my eyes for a second as everyone settled in. All of a sudden I heard several sharp gasps behind me. My head lifted up and my eyes snapped open.

"Jesus Christ!" cried DeAndre. "Look over there!" and he pointed across the street to where Mrs. Carmichael lived alone with her little Scotty dog. An elderly widow, she had lived there forever and everybody in the neighborhood knew her. I swung around and stared, not sure of what I was seeing at first. Then I gasped.

Laid out on the side of Mrs. Carmichael's pristine, manicured Kentucky Bluegrass lawn was what looked like Mrs. Carmichael herself. Three crazies were bent over her, fast at work over her abdomen. She lay perfectly still, and I sent a silent prayer that she was unconscious or dead already. Because those zombies were eating her. From our angle, we could see one of them pull something bloody from her middle and try to chew on it. It sprang back into her and the creature lowered its mouth to my neighbor again. Mrs. Carmichael's Scotty, Blackie, was throwing a fit, growling and barking and trying to grab one of the zombies by the leg and pull it away from her master. They ignored the little dog, but she wouldn't quit. No sooner had one of the creatures shaken her loose than Blackie was back nipping at their heels again, growling insistently in a fruitless attempt to save her mistress. I felt my stomach heave and the gorge rise up to the back of my throat before I was able to swallow it back down again. In the back, the others gasped as they pressed their faces to the windows and watched. Emily turned away almost immediately, her hand holding her mouth and her eyes tightly shut. I didn't blame her. It was impossible to watch. Caitlyn also turned away and they held on to each other and sobbed. Behind Emily, Jacob was fumbling with something in his lap. Suddenly, he jumped up and ran down the aisle and out of the van. Jacob had taken 1st place in the Jr. State Championship SharpShooter trials 3 years running. He poised himself behind the short hood, balancing his father's high-powered Remington rifle against the cold metal and taking aim through the scope.

I held my breath.

POP *POP* The rifle's shots cracked through the quiet morning air. Jacob had hit one of the zombies in the back and head. The second shot took part of its skull with it. The zombie dropped and was still. The others, however, seemed oblivious to what had just happened a few feet away from them. They ignored Jacob – ignored the rifle shots – and kept at Mrs. Carmichael. I could hear them now, faint though they were: growls and slurping sounds. My stomach heaved again, and I rushed out of the van as the bile rose and exited my mouth onto the pavement, my hand still clutching the katana sword.

Jacob had reloaded and was taking aim again.

POP *POP* This time he had hit both of the others in the head.

I looked up just in time to see both of them drop.

"Oh, God," I moaned, still feeling sick. I could hear Emily crying in the van. Jacob grimly pulled the rifle up and looked around.

"Do you see any more?" he asked quietly. I looked around, wiping my mouth. The neighborhood was quiet but eerie.

"No, but it feels like there may be more around," I answered.

DeAndre hopped out of the van. "Where did they come from? I didn't see them when we pulled up," he said.

"I don't know, but I was exhausted. It's not in clear view of Jacob's house. We probably just missed it while we were inside. I think we need to keep a sharper eye out. Fresno is no longer safe," I said.

Jacob turned to me. "Mrs. Carmichael was such a sweet old lady. She brought us pie just last month," he said.

"I know. She was always doing stuff like that for all of us. She's lived on this street for decades. I can't believe what just happened," I said, shaking my head. "If I hadn't seen that with my own eyes I would not have believed it."

Holding his rifle, Jacob walked across the street to the corpse. He bent down briefly to examine it, crouching in the grass. He looked around and up and down the street, into the bushes and through the window of Mrs. Carmichael's house. Everything seemed quiet, like the neighborhood was holding its breath. Then he bent down and scooped up the little black Scotty dog and came back across the street.

"Maybe we can find somewhere where they're fostering animals in the crisis," he said as he stepped into the van. He handed the little dog over to Emily, who was sniffling in her seat halfway back. She took the warm, furry body into her arms and clutched it, smiling. Scooter came up to them and stuck his nose into the little dog's fur. He gave her several licks before settling down at Emily's feet.

As I got in, I paused, looking around the neighborhood again, my hand gripping the long sword. My eyes settled on the still body across the street. Mrs. Carmichael was motionless. Very obviously dead. I blinked back tears as I remembered my neighbor and how she would bake cookies every Christmas and bring them around to everyone in the neighborhood, wrapped in colorful plastic on a plate. She was such a sweet old lady. She didn't deserve this at all. Then I thought about Conner and Coach. They hadn't deserved what happened to them either. I felt tears fill my eyes as I remembered the sight of Conner laid out and attacked by the thing that used to be our teacher. I remember the walls covered in blood that had sprayed when Coach had ripped Conner's throat out and torn out his jugular. The blood would have poured out like a fountain at the end of a pressurized hose. Conner hadn't died right away, his leg had kicked out and his voice had gurgled and he must have known what was happening to him. A shudder went through me. I made a quiet promise to myself that I would find out everything I could about what was going on, and about what had caused this nightmare. I glanced around the rest of the neighborhood. Everything looked clear, so I hopped into the van and settled myself behind the driver's seat again, sword propped up by my leg. I wasn't going to go around unarmed again. My face felt icy cold and I couldn't breathe. I felt numb with shock at what I had seen. The others behind me were silent, except for Emily, who was still crying softly, clutching Blackie in her arms. I was glad Risa hadn't seen Coach and Conner, or Mrs. Carmichael down on her lawn like that. I didn't think I would ever forget those sights, although I wished I could. I took a deep breath and looked at the dashboard clock. It was closing in on 3 p.m. We had been awake for over 24 hours.

Chapter Seven

I took one more look around and turned the key in the ignition. The engine rumbled to life, and I put the van in gear and slowly pulled away from the curb, swinging my head back and forth, trying to see everything at once. After what we had just witnessed, we were definitely in survival mode. I drove quickly through the city streets and made it to the freeway without incident.

In the back of my head something niggled at my thoughts. Where had everyone been evacuated to? I felt a strong pull to my family and wondered where they were right now. On the one hand, I hoped my mother and brother and grandparents had been able to evacuate out of the city to safety. On the other, I hated being separated from them. There was a large part of me that wanted to find out where they were and rush to reunite with them, wherever that may be.

"I wonder where everyone was evacuated to?" I wondered out loud as I pulled onto the freeway. Jacob was behind me, and I half turned my head to him.

"Jacob, take my iPad and try to find out information on where the authorities evacuated Fresno to, okay?" I said. He nodded and got to work. "Thanks," I smiled.

I headed down the 99 south toward Bakersfield. I figured it was the likeliest place to try and reunite with everyone. The trouble had come from the northwest. East had nothing but mountains and the Sequoias. South seemed the most plausible. I didn't know if Bakersfield was still there or if people had moved even farther south, but that was the first large city I would check. I looked down at the gas gauge and saw it was close to being three-quarters empty.

"We're going to need to stop for gas. Okay if we use that money you have, Jacob?" I asked.

"Yeah, that's fine. It's kind of what I brought it for, that and food," he said quietly. "I'm going to check the oil and tires when we stop, too. I don't want to have a breakdown or a flat tire and be stuck somewhere. Things are too crazy. We have to assume the worst."

I nodded. We didn't know what we would encounter, and we had to be ready for anything. Heading south, I looked at the freeway signs and pulled off at the next exit. I knew there were plenty of gas stations off the Jensen exit. As I pulled to a stop at the highway, I looked right and left. Everything looked deserted. I pulled to the left and drove into the gas station and pulled up to a pump. Jacob and I hopped out and soon had gas pumping into the van's tank. I poked my head into the van window.

"Anybody want anything here? Bathroom visit would be good. We're not going to be stopping for a while," I said.

Everyone decided to go into the minimart, so I stayed with Risa. Jacob finished with the gas pump and headed into the store with the others. For a few minutes, it was quiet in the van. I looked down at the sleeping little girl. Her head wound was slightly swollen, but her color and temperature were good. Caitlyn had built a little nest of blankets for her, and she looked so peaceful there. So innocent. I felt an overwhelming need to protect her. To protect them all. I sighed and smoothed her hair against her cheek.

DeAndre and Emily were hopping back into the van right then, so I got up to take my turn at the bathroom.

"Everything look okay?" I asked. They both nodded tiredly.

Entering the store, I greeted the clerk and then made my way to the side bathrooms. Afterwards, I grabbed a couple of energy drinks and brought them up to counter.

"Hey, do you have any word on the evacuations? Where did everybody get directed to?" I asked.

"Bakersfield mostly, although some went to Los Angeles. It's crazy. I'm splitting at the end of my shift. I stayed only because I'm waiting for my wife and her brother to join me before I leave. If we got split up, who knows when we'd get back together again?" he said.

I nodded and grabbed my purchases and headed back to the van. As I approached it, I saw that Jacob was checking the oil. I put my drinks in the van and then went to get the tire gauge out of the glove box. Jacob went back into the store and came out a few minutes later with a bottle of oil for the engine. I checked the tires, and they all looked pretty good. I packed the gauge back into the van and went to check on Jacob's progress. He was just closing the hood as I walked around to him.

"I'm just going to go wash my hands?" he said. I nodded and he went back into the store. I looked around again. No cars were on these roads, which were normally pretty heavily trafficked at this time of day. It was eerie. I couldn't wait to get back on the road and out of this city. I had had enough. I heard a noise and turned. Jacob was coming back. The sound I heard had been the sound of him coming through the door. I must be getting jumpy, I thought. I shook my head and got back into the driver's seat as he hopped into the van and settled into the seat behind me.

"Alyssa, when you get too tired, let me drive?" he said as he drank a bottle of water. "We should all share the burden of driving, especially with what's been going on."

I nodded. "I think I'll be okay for a while, I've got these, I don't think I'll crash anytime soon," I said as I held up one of the energy drinks. I popped the top and took a long sip of the frosty cold drink, then turned again to the front and settled in, setting my drink in the nearby cup holder and buckling my seatbelt. I started the van and pulled out of the gas station. Heading down the freeway again, I felt better. Our van was all gassed up, oil in and tires checked. All of us had gotten drinks and visited the bathroom. I could hear Emily, Caitlyn and DeAndre talking quietly behind me, and Jacob was again looking on the iPad.

Nothing felt as if it were real; it almost seemed like a nightmare. I shook my head and surreptitiously pinched my arm, wincing as pain flooded my head. *Well,* I thought, *at least I'm as awake as I'm going to get.* I grimaced and kept driving. It was a straight shot, a lonely drive south towards the bigger city of Bakersfield. In between Fresno and Bakersfield was a series of smaller towns. I debated on stopping in one of them. Looking briefly behind me, I saw that everyone had settled down for the two-hour long drive and no one was restless. I decided on trying to push through to the bigger city, through the flat stretches of agricultural land on either side of the freeway. There wasn't much in those smaller towns, anyway. Tulare. Delano. Their names all ran together on the map. With my luck, they were already deserted anyway. I sighed tiredly and set the cruise control on the van to 70 mph. The two-lane southbound 99 freeway was mostly surrounded by various agricultural lands, and the miles passed by quickly. I had already been driving nearly an hour when I heard a commotion behind me, and someone cried out.

"What's going on back there, Jacob?" I asked, looking behind me. But Jacob had already unbuckled his seatbelt and made his way to the back of the van. I glanced behind me again briefly but couldn't see anything. I slowed down to a stop at the edge of the freeway.

As I put the van in park and turned the key to remove it, Emily came up to the front.

"Alyssa, Risa is awake and she needs to go to the bathroom. I've given her some ibuprofen and a Coke, but she's says she's really uncomfortable and hungry. Is there anywhere we can stop ahead?"

"We're almost up to Tulare, I'll pull over there. Tell her it'll be about 10 more minutes?" I said. She nodded and made her way back to the others. I could hear crying in the back. Risa must have noticed Conner and Coach were missing.

I soon pulled off the freeway and turned down a main road. Half a mile down from the freeway was an open am/pm store and Arco station. It looked like there were a few people there, so I turned into the driveway. I pulled up to a parking place, we were still pretty full on gas and could easily make it to Bakersfield and even Los Angeles if we had to. As I pulled up and stopped the van, I noticed a very pregnant woman on the walkway outside the store. She was tall and appeared to be in her twenties. And she looked very pregnant. We piled out of the van, and Emily and Caitlyn took Risa in to the bathroom while DeAndre, Jacob and I stood around outside waiting. The pregnant woman was talking to a guy who was on his way back out to his vehicle. I heard him say, "I told you: no, I can't help. We're already loaded up past capacity," before he walked on to an old overloaded station wagon where I could see at least five kids, a woman, and two dogs, as well as numerous pieces of luggage and various boxes. The pregnant woman turned away from him, looking worried. Then she saw us and came toward us.

"Please, can you help me with a ride? My husband was killed and my car broke down about a mile east of here. Look, see? I can pay," she said as she held out a handful of bills." Her face looked nearly desperate. I looked her over. She looked like she had been well taken care of at one time, but it looked as if the last couple of days had been trying for her. She wore what appeared to be a designer dress, though it was a bit dirty from her ordeal, and her mannerisms seemed cultured as well. She was wearing expensive shoes, too. Tears filled her eyes as she pleaded again. "I've been trying to get someone to help me for over an hour, everyone's too loaded up or too busy to listen. We missed the evacuations day before yesterday, and last night we were attacked while we slept in our apartment. Jack was killed trying to protect me." At this she broke down and sobbed. "He died. It was aw ...awful!" her voice hiccupped. "I got into our car and started driving but I hit some rubble and the tires went flat. I dragged my suitcase over a mile to this place. Please help me! I promise not to burden you. All I want is a ride to safety!" she finished.

My god. We had plenty of room in our van, and she looked to be free from the disease. I wasn't about to let her stay here. As I stepped forward, DeAndre had already moved past me and to the woman.

"Of course we'll help you," he said as he picked up her suitcase. "What's your name?"

"Oh my God, thank you! My name is Holly White. Thank you so much!"

Jacob opened up the door as DeAndre lifted her suitcase into the van.

"Are you hungry or thirsty? Do you need to visit the bathroom? We'll be heading out pretty soon." I said.

Holly looked tearful but happy. "I guess I should go wash up and maybe get some water."

DeAndre walked into the store with Holly. I turned to Jacob.

"She looks close to term. I wonder when she's due?" I said.

"I'm not sure, I don't know much about babies and women. I can't believe nobody else would help her. Do you think she'll be all right with us? You don't think she's dangerous, do you? We don't know her or anything." Jacob said.

I thought for a moment. "I guess we'll find out. We're taking a chance, but I'll be damned if I leave a pregnant woman out in the cold. That baby she's carrying didn't ask for this, and I know I'd want someone to help my mom if she'd been in this situation," I replied. Jacob nodded his head silently.

Just then, Caitlyn, Emily and Risa came out. Risa looked much better and was chowing down on a couple of Twinkies. I smiled. "Feeling a little better, kiddo?" I asked.

Risa smiled through her full mouth and nodded happily. Kids were so resilient. Except for a bruise on her forehead, she looked none the worse for wear. I gave her a hug and helped her back into the van while Jacob brought Emily and Caitlyn up to speed on the Holly situation. I decided to let the dogs out onto the side grass next to our van. They happily relieved themselves and drank thirstily out of the bucket of water put there for dogs. Ten minutes later we were all packed back into the van. Holly was settled in the middle and DeAndre was talking animatedly with her. Jacob was behind me again, and Emily and Caitlyn were with Risa and the two dogs toward the back. I turned on the engine and pulled back onto the southbound 99 freeway toward Bakersfield. After driving for ten minutes I tried the radio. Nothing but static on every channel. I was worried. Bakersfield stations should be coming in, unless they've evacuated that city too.

Chapter Eight

"Jacob, do you see any news for Bakersfield on Twitter or CNN or anything? I can't pick up a single radio station," I asked over my shoulder.

"Um, let's see…" he scrolled through Twitter again, adding the #bakersfield hashtag. "Nothing so far. Let me try Google," he said.

"Thanks. I would really love to know what kind of situation we're driving into before we get there," I said.

"Me too," he said. After a pause, he continued, "I see nothing really recent on Bakersfield. Something from last night says the police were telling everyone to stay inside and not go out at all." He sighed. "Man, that would drive me crazy. Just sitting there in a house waiting for something to happen. Who knows what could come into the neighborhood? You'd just be a sitting duck," he said.

"Well," I said, "let's just hope the hospital is still running. We should get Risa's head wound checked out. I'm worried that she was out for so long, although it was a blessing that she missed all the stuff that happened."

Jacob nodded and returned to his search. As I drove, I looked around. The local roads alongside the freeway were deserted. There was no traffic going north, and just a few cars were headed south with us. When we got to Bakersfield, we headed straight for the Kern Medical Center. But as we pulled up into the big emergency room area, I saw the parking lot was mostly deserted: not a good sign at all, I thought. I parked and set the brake, turning to face the others.

"Guys, I don't like the look of this. But maybe people were evacuated. Either way, I'd like to try and see if we can get Risa checked out. Maybe get some news on the evacuations. Who is coming with me and who is staying in the van?"

It turned out no one was willing to split up, so we all went in, leaving the dogs in the van alone. We took our weapons with us, just in case. As we got out, I looked quickly back and forth but saw nothing irregular. The seven of us made a scraggly group as we walked across the parking lot and through the double doors of the hospital. The inside of the hospital seemed deserted. I led us down the corridor calling out, "hello's" every dozen feet or so. Finally, a haggard-looking nurse peeked out at us from behind a mostly closed door.

"Are they gone?" she asked, looking up and down the corridor. At this, I began to feel a prickly sensation as the hairs on the back of my neck rose.

"What do you mean?" I asked. "We just drove down from Fresno. We have an injured little girl with us. What's been going on here?"

"Do you have any doctors available?" Jacob asked, looking around as he spoke.

Before she could respond, my thoughts were jolted by the sound of screaming. It was coming from the end of the corridor, where we had come in. Whipping around to look, we saw another nurse running. Behind her were three people. They were running after her, but staggering as they ran. One was a man in a business suit with what looked like half his face covered in blood. One was a woman in a torn blouse who was dragging her left leg, which was also bloody. The third I couldn't make out clearly until I looked again. Then I gasped in horror. The man's scalp was torn half off, and it hung down over the side of his face and flapped as he ran after the nurse. They all had the same dark grey skin color as the others had had, and they were coming toward us. Fast. The nurse they were chasing screamed as the man in the business suit caught up to her and grabbed at her. She fell heavily to the ground and skidded a few yards, then scrambled to her feet as the zombies reached for her. She was fast and although they grabbed for her, and got hold of her sweater, she ran on and peeled the sweater off as she ran. It came off of her and the zombies tore it apart with their teeth, but that gave the nurse the seconds she need to sprint away.

The nurse who had opened the door to talk to us cried out, "Stacy!" and screamed, "Run! They're coming again!" as the three crazed zombies took up the chase once more. As the nurse called Stacy ran toward us, the other nurse who had called out to her gasped and disappeared behind the door again. We heard a growl very close to us, and as we watched as a zombie with yellow pus running down her face grabbed the nurse from behind. She had been in the room with her all along. Behind us, three more zombies came through the doors we had just entered. This all happened in less than a minute.

Jacob grabbed my arm and yelled, "Come on, guys!" then began to run down the length of the other corridor. DeAndre scooped up Risa, and we all ran together away from the chaos behind us. The corridor swerved to the right, and we soon came upon a bank of elevators. There was another corridor off to the left that looked deserted.

"Which way?" I cried. As if in answer, we heard a growl coming from the left corridor and what sounded like someone slapping against a wall. Not waiting to see what had made that noise, I pulled us all into the alcove and punched the elevator buttons repeatedly. Nothing happened. Elevators always took so long. My heart raced, and adrenaline flooded my system. The nurse running from the three crazed zombies had nearly reached us, but the creature that had once been a businessman was right behind her. As she ran up to us, he grabbed her hair from behind and yanked her off her feet. Screaming, she flipped backward just as the elevator doors opened. We piled inside as she screamed, the man clawing at her face. Blood was everywhere. Making sure we were all inside, I frantically punched the floor buttons, but it seemed to take an eternity for the doors to close.

Meanwhile, the zombie had lowered his face to the nurse called Stacy and began to bite her. The other two zombies ran up right then; one fell beside the man and started biting the nurse's arm. She screamed again and struggled all the more frantically. The businessman jumped on top of her knees first and held her down, and her screams began to sound liquidy. The third zombie ran up and tried to grab one of her flailing legs, but she kicked him. Dazed, he looked up at us just as the doors to the elevator began to close. He seemed to sense prey – to sense us – and lunged at the doors. His arm came through as the elevator doors finished closing, but the sensor detected an obstacle, and they began to open again. Risa screamed, and Jacob kicked at the intruder. My breath caught in my throat. DeAndre landed a kick at the zombie's midsection which threw him off balance. He fell backward, landing across the threshold. Jacob grabbed his legs and flung them out as I pressed the floor button again. Suddenly the zombie, flailing on his back as he tried to right himself, let out a scream so piercing it seemed almost supersonic. I gasped. I had never heard such a sound issue forth from a human being before. The doors began to close again just as the thing rolled over and got to its feet. As he turned toward us again, the doors closed on the sight of him reaching out in our direction, grasping and flailing at the air. But this time, he was an inch too far away, and the doors closed before he managed to reach us. As we began to ascend, we heard him screaming in frustration and pounding on the metal doors that had just closed.

Breathing hard, we checked each other for wounds.

"My God!" cried Holly, clutching her round belly, "Oh my God!!"

Risa sobbed in the corner in Emily's arms. Caitlyn's face was ashen. Jacob and DeAndre were breathing hard. I looked at the buttons. There were five floors. I wanted to get us as far away from the madness as I could, so I pressed "5" for the top floor. As the elevator passed the second and third floors, we could hear more screaming. The sounds faded as we passed the third and fourth floors, and finally the elevator stopped at the fifth. It was silent as the doors quietly opened. I cautiously looked out, my senses on alert. Who knew what we would encounter?

"Be careful," Caitlyn whispered as Jacob poked his head out the doors. I pressed and held the "open door" button so the elevator wouldn't close on him. We didn't hear anything except our own heavy breathing and Risa's quiet hiccups, so I stepped out onto the floor. Looking up and down the corridor, I saw nothing. Everything was as still as death. Jacob stepped out beside me and looked around too. I motioned for the others to come, and we silently stepped into the middle of the corridor. The elevator doors began to close but I wanted to keep the thing there. Not only as an escape route, but I didn't want zombies piling in and riding up to meet us.

"Hold it open for a minute, DeAndre," I said. I walked a dozen feet down the corridor, grabbed a clipboard from the nurse's station there and returned. DeAndre saw what I was doing and stepped out of the elevator, holding the doors open with his hand. Placing the big, boxy clipboard on the floor in the middle, I waited for the doors to begin closing, and made sure it held the doors a few inches open. I hoped it would work. It seemed to do the trick.

"Which way should we try?" Caitlyn asked, looking up and down the hall. My eyes followed hers, first in one direction, then the other. It looked utterly deserted, but as I looked closer, I could see that the chair at the nurse's station had been overturned and supplies were scattered all over the floor. It looked as if there had been a struggle, but there was no way of telling where the combatants had gone.

I looked up as Jacob whispered, "I smell smoke."

I sniffed the air. Sure enough, there was a faint scent of smoke. "Where is that smell coming from?"

"I think it's coming from this way," Emily said, pointing behind her and away from the elevator. I walked a few feet down the corridor she indicated. She was right: the smoke smelled just a bit stronger down this way. Still faint, but unmistakable.

"Let's go this way, then," I said as I started down the opposite way. As we passed the elevators, the air cleared completely. "The fire alarm system must be out," I said quietly, looking up at the fire system sprinklers. "With smoke or fire, those things should be on and drenching us."

A fire alarm system in a hospital failing? That didn't seem right. Medical centers always doubled up on safety precautions. As we continued down the corridor, I added the mystery of the nonfunctional fire alarms to the list of questions in my head. Hopefully soon, we would have some answers.

The corridor dead ended at an intersection.

"Which way now?" asked Holly.

One way seemed as good a choice as the other, so I randomly picked the right hand side and began to lead the group cautiously down the hallway, pausing at each door and listening. After passing about six doors, I listened at the seventh. It was closed, but I could hear voices coming from the other side. At least two people were behind the door engaged in a conversation of some sort, speaking softly as though were trying to avoid detection. Their tone was deliberate, rather than agitated. I knocked hesitantly, and the voices stopped. I put my face at the crack between the door and the wall and said, "Hey. Anybody in there?" After a minute, the door cracked open an inch. A man's face appeared, and he looked us up and down.

"Who are you? Is it safe out there?" he asked.

"It's safe. We're alone. We just drove down from Fresno. We have a little girl who has a head injury. We tried the Emergency Room but got chased and ended up in an elevator. We came up here. Can we come in there? Kinda feel like sitting ducks out here."

He nodded and opened the door to what turned out to be an office, and we followed him inside. Two women were there in the room with him. One of them wore a hospital uniform, as did the man. The other woman was in street clothes.

There weren't enough chairs for all seven of us, so we all settled down on the floor. "Is any of you a doctor? Risa hit her head so hard she was unconscious most of the day," I said, bringing Risa forward.

The woman in street clothes stepped forward. "I'm a doctor," she said, beginning to examine Risa. "When did she hit her head?"

"It was this morning around 8," Emily said. "She fell and hit her head on the floor at Saint Agnes in Fresno." She moved forward to hold Risa's hand while the doctor examined her head.

Jacob turned his attention to the other two people. "Do you know what's been going on?" he asked. "We just got in from across the country last night."

The man nodded. "I know what happened. My wife has a sister who worked at Stanford in the Literature Department. My name's

Mike, by the way." He reached out to shake our hands, one by one. "My wife passed away last year, and I am really glad I kept in touch with her family. I found out what happened only two weeks ago, when I talked to them on the phone."

Worked. I knew Stanford had been under some sort of attack. Still, to hear him speak in the past tense like that was jarring.

"This all started roughly three years ago," he said. "My sister-in-law was working at Stanford when they sent a team to Europe. They'd uncovered the mass graves where the victims of the Black Plague had been buried. When they opened the graves, they found out that the bodies had been just dumped there by the hundreds and thousands, without any caskets or preparation. It looked like it had all happened very quickly."

"They also could tell that some of the victims had been buried alive. Some of them seem to have been trying to claw their way out."

Our faces were masks of horror, mixed with incredulity.

He continued.

"They found that the survivors had dumped the bodies, most dead, but some still alive, and had covered them up with dirt and rocks as fast as they could. In light of what's happening, this might have tipped them off about what to expect. But you know scientists. Anyway, when they exhumed these bodies, they found that the bone marrow in some of the victims was still intact. Now, keep in mind this all happened back in the mid-1300s. These bodies should have been dust, and some were. But the scientists found a healthy minority with intact bone marrow."

"So they took this marrow back to the labs at Stanford and found that they could reawaken the illness that killed these people."

We gasped at the implications.

"Now, today, we do have a strain of the Black Plague that we can cure. It's a bacteria called *Yersinia Pestis*. With modern medicine, antibiotics and such, plus a clean, sterile hospital environment, this strain of the infection can be cured. But. …"

"Aha," I mumbled, thinking, there's always a 'but'.

Mike smiled at me and continued. "So the scientists probably weren't too worried when they began using the bone marrow to reawaken the 14th century version of the Black Plague. My sister-in-law explained it to me, about two weeks ago. The 14th century strain of the worst pandemic in history, because after all, it killed off over half the population. Well, it wasn't the same as the modern day version. Turns out our 21st century strain is quite the watered down version of *Yersinia Pestis*. Seven centuries ago, what they were hit by was apparently a very virulent strain of the bacteria. A strain that, even today, we really cannot fight." He sat back, looking into our faces.

"What's worse? The 14th century strain of the Black Plague seems to turn its victims into raving lunatics who attack anyone they can. That's how it's spread. Through bites, body fluids, any way it can get into your bloodstream, it will. And," he continued, apparently the worst was not over yet, "This highly contagious strain of Plague escaped the lab at Stanford about three days ago. California is in the beginnings of a pandemic it probably cannot survive. Travel is hugely different nowadays. This thing will probably spread fast, and there's not much they can do about it." He fell silent and closed his eyes.

Paula spoke up. "We must take great care to keep from being bitten or scratched, but we must also keep all infected fluids off of us. This is not like HIV. It's much more contagious. This thing spreads easily and can survive in any moist environment; even getting a smear of fluid on a cut you got the day before can infect you."

"This plague killed off 100 million people in an era when most people lived their whole lives in the small villages where they were born, rarely venturing more than a few miles away. In this modern day and age, where a deadly illness is just a plane ride away from any continent on the planet, it could wipe out all human life on Earth."

Chapter Nine

"Oh my god," said Jacob. Everyone was silent for a while. My face felt numb. I looked at Jacob and his face was white in shock.

"...I guess we're finding out why those mass graves were so hastily dug. And so deeply buried," I said. "I wonder if the authorities are close to getting a handle on this problem or if the whole West Coast is still just in flight mode."

"Does anyone know if these crazies – the people who have been infected – are organized?" Jacob asked. "They seem to act randomly most of the time."

"But they also team up against their victims. They don't seem to be territorial," DeAndre observed.

"They're almost acting like a pack of wild dogs," Emily said.

I remembered Mrs. Carmichael and the nurse down on the bottom floor. Why had the second zombie left the nurse's body and lunged for us? Wasn't the body enough to satiate the zombies down there? Why did it come for us? It was almost as if they were acting like hungry animals.

"They're not just looking for food," I said. "That nurse on the first floor should have been enough for all the zombies down there. But that one tried to attack us in the elevator. It was aggressive."

Mike looked up sharply. "The elevator? Did it come up with you to this floor?" he asked.

"No, we got away and I left a clipboard propping the door open so the elevator would stay up here in the fifth floor," I said, still feeling numb. "What's the situation on this floor?" I asked.

"We've been here since about 6 a.m.," Mike said. "There was an outbreak early this morning. When I got on duty, there was chaos on the first floor."

"My name is Dr. Paula Cordial. I'm an anesthesiologist. I got here at a little past 5 a.m. and there were patients being brought in from Fresno and Clovis. They were contagious and seemed near death. Then all of a sudden they turned into those things. Zombies did you call them? Black Plague victims." said the doctor.

"Zombies seem to be as accurate a description as we've got," I answered. "They catch this disease, get really sick, get near death, and then turn into these creatures. They turn grey, then black, they have great strength, they don't speak, they attack humans. Sounds very close to what the legends say zombies are like."

"They say all myths and legends have some basis in fact," Jacob added quietly.

"Do you think these zombies existed in the 14th century and then just died off? Or did they kill them all off," asked Caitlyn.

"They probably killed them off," Jacob said. "There weren't that many people around in the 14th century, and after the Black Plague killed off half the population of Europe, there wouldn't have been many people left in the countryside. Just those who had weapons and were good fighters, to defend themselves," Jacob said.

"Or those who were immune," I added quietly. I turned to the last woman in the room. She had been quiet the whole time. She seemed to be an older woman, and she was in some kind of uniform. "Hi, what's your name?" I asked.

"My name is Ellie. I work the receptionist desk in the Emergency Room," she answered.

Mike smiled. "Ellie is a very fast runner."

I nodded. "So you all have been here for the whole day? Were there zombies on this floor when you came in this room?"

Dr. Cordial nodded, finishing her examination of Risa. "She's going to be okay. She has a slight concussion and swelling on her head, but her skull doesn't seem to be fractured. Her temperature is good, and she seems to be alert now. She's a tough little girl." She turned to face us. "We were chased down this hallway from the stairwell at the end of the corridor."

"At the end of the right side corridor?" Jacob asked.

"Yes. Did you come that way?" Mike asked.

"No, we came from the left, from down the corridor with the elevator," I answered. "It was quiet in the hallway when we came up to your door."

"Do you have any water?" Emily asked.

Paula nodded and reached into the drawer of the desk. She pulled out some water bottles and passed them around. "This is actually a colleague's office." She wrapped her arms around herself and shivered. "I wish I knew where everyone was. This hospital should be full of people. This hallway is never silent: there's always voices and bustling up and down it at all hours."

"It *is* very quiet. Too quiet," Mike said.

We finished our waters and tried to relax for the next ten minutes or so. But I couldn't. I was restless.

"I can't stay in here. I've got to make some progress. We need to get back to our van," I said, grabbing my katana sword and standing up. Jacob and Caitlyn rose with me. Emily struggled to her feet, helping Holly with Risa. Paula nodded, and Mike and Ellie gathered their things as we prepared to start moving.

Jacob opened the door quietly and peeked out. The corridor was deserted. The smell of smoke had grown stronger, but we could still see clearly. I looked down the right hand side, toward the stairwell where Paula said the zombies had chased them. I led the way down to the left, back toward the elevators.

"Is there another stairwell on this floor?" I whispered.

"Yes. Past the elevators at the other end of the floor," Paula said.

Back where the smoke was coming from, I noted. Well, we would try. I walked down to the intersection and turned left again toward the elevators and the trashed nurses' station. Everyone followed me. I held my katana steadily, end pointed down, ready for anything. I got as far as the elevator and stopped, listening. Everyone came to a stop behind me, silent. I could hear an alarm sounding far away: it sounded like it was coming from several floors below us. Other than that, it was quiet. Too quiet for a hospital. I continued past the nurses' station, and on to the end of the corridor. It ended in a "T".

"Which way?" I asked.

"Left," whispered Paula right at my back. I almost jumped. I looked back and she was almost on top of me.

"Figured I'd stay next to the leader with the sword," she said, smiling grimly. I nodded and gestured for the rest to follow. We were a tight group, slowly creeping forward, listening for anything. I turned left and walked another 50 yards or so, and everyone followed me. They were quiet and alert. When we reached the end of the corridor, our way was barred by a closed door. I turned to the others.

"I'm going to check the stairwell. Be ready," I said, looking into their eyes. I saw fear there, and fatigue, along with a grim resolve. I suspected they could see the same in my eyes. It was a bad feeling, being trapped in this building. I couldn't wait until we were out of here and back in the van driving down the road. I was willing to bet the others felt the same. We were on the top floor, with nowhere to go but down. . It felt desperate, being boxed in like this. I slowly opened the door a crack, looking and listening.

Before I could figure out whether it was safe or not, we all heard a faint but distinct growling coming from behind us.

Chapter Ten

"Oh my God," Caitlyn whispered. She and Risa were at the rear of the group, and faced whatever was coming first. A chill went down my spine. The growl was joined by a second growl and then a crash. It sounded like it had come from just beyond the last turn of the corridor. We all looked behind us and Jacob silently grabbed Risa's left hand, while DeAndre grabbed her right.

Suddenly, we heard running and stumbling. A man came around the corner, quickly followed by a woman. They were both in the advanced stages of the plague, and their faces were nearly black. They staggered ahead slowly, their faces lowered as they growled. Then they seemed to smell us, and looked up.

The instant I saw them, I opened the stairwell door and began pushing the others through without a sound. I got three of them through before the two zombies noticed us. Then I shouted, "Come on!"

In a split second there was utter chaos. Everyone piled into the stairwell as I held the door open, then Jacob took the door while I screamed and made as much sound as I could, trying to scare, or at least confuse the zombies. I flailed my arms and waved my katana, screaming like a wild girl. It did the trick. The two creatures seemed shocked, and just stood there for a few seconds, hesitating. That gave me enough time to get everyone through the door. Just as Jacob grabbed my arm to pull me through, the two zombies began to charge. The distance between us was about 40 yards, and they were *fast.* I barely had time to get myself through the door with my sword, and Jacob slammed it fast. Unfortunately, it didn't have a lock – only a push-bar lever on the other side. As the door slammed shut, Jacob leaned his body against it hard. A second later, one of the zombies slammed into the lever on the other side, and the door bounced open a half-inch before Jacob braced himself against the concrete. The others had run down to the level below. I pushed myself against the door next to Jacob, and a second later DeAndre threw his weight against the door as well. The zombies growled and pounded on the door, but with the three of us holding it, the door didn't budge. Still, we were stuck.

The others slowly crept halfway back up to us and waited on the stairs, looking scared. The growls continued, and the zombies were pounding on the door insistently. Jacob, DeAndre and I grimly pushed back. The noise of them pounding on the door was very loud, and I was worried it might attract the attention of other zombies.

"Caitlyn," I said quietly. "Go down one floor and listen at the door. See if the coast is clear on that floor, okay?" I said. She nodded and left to go check, taking Holly with her. Emily held Risa's hand. Risa looked scared and clutched Emily's hand like a lifeline. Mike and Paula stood a few feet away with Ellie, looking scared, waiting to see what would happen. The three of us stayed where we were, our full weight bracing the door, for about 10 minutes. Caitlyn came back and said the corridor seemed clear but smoky. The fire was probably on the second floor. Not a good place for us to be. But this stairwell was a death trap if we were caught in here.

This thought had no sooner filled my brain than I heard a new noise. It was a scrambling and growling, coming from the other side of the door. The two zombies seemed to be fighting each other. They had left the door alone for a minute and were loudly growling and screaming at each other. I looked at Jacob and nodded. With luck, they had forgotten us behind the door in their fight with each other. I looked up the stairwell.

"Where does that go?" I asked Mike.

"To the roof," he said.

I wanted to know all my options. I made a decision, nodded at Jacob and DeAndre, and then we quietly, but quickly ran down the stairwell. We made it down one landing, and as I passed the door, I pressed my hand against it. It was hot.

"There's fire behind that door," I whispered.

We made it to the bottom floor, and I listened against the door. I heard some quiet scratching noises. I didn't know what they were, but I wanted out of that stairwell. I cracked the door open.

As I put my eye to the one-inch crack and peered out. The sight that met my eyes was one of the most shocking I'd ever had. I let out and involuntary scream.

In the hallway outside the door were five zombies, all feeding on a small child, and the child was still alive. She thrashed weakly on the floor as the zombies chewed on her arms and legs. They didn't appear to have hit a major artery, so it looked like she was going to bleed to death slowly while they ate her. At the sound of my scream, they all looked up. Four of the zombies jumped for the door. They were about 5 feet away, and I instinctively jumped back as their black hands reached for the crack in the door.

"Oh my God!" I cried and fell backward. Jacob grabbed for the door to pull it shut. But it was too late. The four zombies threw all their weight on the door at once and forced it open, stumbling into the stairwell. Caitlyn screamed. Jacob raised his shotgun and leveled it at the zombies, but they pushed it aside in the close quarters and reached their arms for Emily, who was between Jacob and me. Before any of us could react much, the first zombie had lowered its face to Emily's head and bit down.

Emily screamed in terror and, in the same moment, I raised my sword and brought it down on the zombie's shoulders. The sharp katana sliced through half the creature's neck and arm and made it stop and look up. DeAndre grabbed Emily and pulled her up the stairwell, following everyone else who was rushing upward in a blind panic.

Jacob brought his shotgun up again and blasted it into the second zombie's chest. He hit point blank, sending it back on its heels and halfway out the door where it fell on its back, blocking the door open. The zombie that had bitten Emily rose up again and came at me. I brought the sword down again, this time cleaving his head clean off. The head bounced down the stairs, and the body fell to the ground.

The other two zombies then came through the door together, and Jacob fired the shotgun. The blast was deafening. The zombies were so close together in the confined space of the stairwell that the shot hit them both in the head, taking parts of their skulls with it. They dropped to the ground. The zombie Jacob had shot first was somehow getting to its feet, and the fifth zombie had left the now-motionless girl and was coming through behind it.

"I need to reload!" cried Jacob.

"Get behind me!" I said, and swung my katana sword again.

I had almost swung too quickly, but the end of the sword cleaved through top two inches of the zombie's head and held fast. The zombie slowly fell to its knees, taking my sword with it.

The last zombie growled behind it and tried to climb over him to get at me. All of a sudden, DeAndre came up next to me and kicked the last zombie full in the chest. It fell backward into the hallway. I worked at my sword, trying to get it free. As the last zombie began to crawl back toward me, I finally put my foot on the body of the zombie my sword was stuck in and gave a great heave and my sword came loose. Just in time, I swung it up and back down, cleaving the head from the body on the last zombie. The head rolled back into the hallway and the body fell forward on top of his comrade.

Breathing hard, I grasped my sword and look past them into the hallway. It seemed clear. I called over my shoulder, "Come on!"

We all piled out of the stairwell, stepping over the bodies of the zombies and passed the body of the now-dead little girl they had been feasting on when we opened the door. Jacob had reloaded his shotgun again and held it at the ready. Paula and DeAndre carried Emily, who was unconscious. Caitlyn and Holly had Risa, and Mike and Ellie brought up the rear.

I wanted to get us out of there as soon as possible. As I crept down the hallway toward the door, I could hear screaming from the other end of the corridor. Tears ran down my face as I looked back at Emily, her head was bleeding freely. Paula was trying the staunch the flow, but her blood was dripping out onto the floor. I turned around and began to jog down the corridor. We had to get out of there now, before more zombies came and attacked us. As we turned a corner, in front of us was another zombie, a female. She had just turned, because she her skin was still normal flesh color.

"Sweet Jesus! Trisha!" cried Mike.

Trisha the zombie swung her vacant eyes toward Mike and stumbled forward. Risa screamed, and I brought my sword up to swing it, but Jacob beat me to it with a deafening shotgun blast that took off Trisha's face and most of her head, and echoed down the corridor. She fell backward to the ground without a sound. Mike sobbed as we ran past.

As the doors to the parking lot came into view, three more zombies stumbled after us from another direction. I hit the doors at a near sprint, the others were right behind me. Risa's feet weren't even on the ground as DeAndre lifted her up by the hand as he ran. We ran out onto the parking lot and I looked wildly around. We had exited into a different place than we had entered.

"Quick, which way is the Emergency Room parking lot?" I cried.

"This way," Mike answered, running off to the right. We ran around the corner and, after a minute, the van came into view. Unfortunately, so did four more zombies. They were stumbling at us from the gas station across the street. Stumbling but still moving fast. They were going to cut us off. DeAndre threw Emily across his shoulder, and we took off toward the van. Jacob fired his shotgun at the zombies, trying to stop them in their paths. It worked, sort of. They paused for a second or two, confused. It gave us the time we needed to get to the van. I unlocked it and yelled, "Everyone in! Come on!"

I looked wildly around us. Zombies were running at us from several directions a few blocks away, but the four zombies closest to us were almost to the van. Jacob fired again and hit one of them hard enough to take it down. But the three others kept coming. They were about ten feet away when I jumped into the open van, just ahead of Jacob. He slammed the door just as the zombies reached us, their arms and faces slamming against the windows.

I scrambled into the driver's seat and fumbled with the key. My hand was shaking, and it took several tries to find the ignition.

"There's more coming!" screamed Caitlyn. I swung my head around to the left as the engine roared to life. There looked to be a dozen figures stumbling toward us.

"Oh, sweet Jesus!" I mumbled. One of the people running was a young woman who was trying to stay ahead of the zombies. But they were right behind her. As the other zombies slammed into the glass on the right again, I began to drive slowly away. The zombies ran after the van, hitting it with their fists. As I drove out of the parking lot and onto the street, the woman saw us and veered towards us. Two steps behind her was a group of three zombies, and they were gaining on her. I looked into her panicked eyes.

"PLEASE! HELP ME!" She screamed. I drew in a swift breath as I watched. She was still 50 yards from us when the first zombie caught her and they went down in a heap. As we drove nearer, the other two zombies fell onto the woman, who was screaming and thrashing. It was too late: her body all but disappeared beneath a mass of hungry grey-black flesh. I sobbed as I drove passed.

Other zombies began appearing and running toward us. Some ran to the woman on the ground, and soon a dozen of them were on her. As we drove down the street toward the freeway, at least fifteen of them ran after us. I accelerated and left them behind. I pulled onto the freeway going south.

Chapter Eleven

"Jacob," I said quietly. He came up to me. "How is Emily?" I asked.

"Not good. She's still unconscious. Paula got the bleeding stopped, but she lost a lot of blood. She's very pale. And Alyssa. She was bitten. She's infected," Jacob said quietly.

Tears sprung to my eyes. "Take care of her. Keep her comfortable and warm," I said. He nodded and made his way to the rear again. I drove on. I tried to concentrate on driving, but tears dropped silently from my eyes as the sun set. Driving on the freeway toward Los Angeles, my friend dying in the back seat. A sob broke out as I tried to wipe my eyes clear of tears. Thankfully, the freeway was empty of cars. It seemed as though we were alone in the world. I could hear Caitlyn crying softly in the back, and DeAndre comforting her. Risa joined in on the crying, I heard Scooter and the little Scottie dog whining, and Jacob came up to the driver's area.

"Emily is getting worse," he said grimly, sitting down beside me. "Paula is trying to help her, but there's nothing she can do about the infection." He sniffed quietly and I glanced at him. Tears were running silently down his face. Seeing him cry made my tears double. I let out a soft moan of sadness.

"Emily and I had English together last term," I said. "I helped her finish her midterm essay. It was on her dreams for her future. She wanted to be a ballet dancer."

Jacob mumbled something inaudible and stared out the window.

I couldn't believe it. Not Emily. She was so sweet, the gentlest of my friends. The tears kept coming. I blew my nose.

As I drove, my head filled with memories of Emily. The fun we had had in New York, all of us seeing a Broadway play, sightseeing at the Statue of Liberty, running through pigeons in Central Park on a perfect day. She was such a good friend. She didn't deserve any of this. Lost in memories, I drove on. After about an hour, I came to the Flying J, a truck stop on the way to Los Angeles. I decided to stop, refuel and check on Emily.

I tried to look ahead as I put my foot on the brake and pulled off the freeway. It had to be safe. We had been through so much already. I looked at the gas gauge, it was nearly three-quarters empty. Driving slowly down the side road and turning into the parking lot, everything looked calm. Just one car in the parking lot and the lights on inside. I could see the clerk as I pulled into a parking place; he was moving about normally.

Without a word, I turned the van off and got out. The rest were silent and came with me, with the exception of Paula, who stayed with Emily. We filed in, and I nodded to the clerk as I turned left toward the bathrooms. He nodded back. The place was safe.

After I finished at the bathroom, I went and gathered some snacks and then headed toward the aisle that had Band-Aids and aspirin. I gathered up anything I thought might help Paula make Emily more comfortable and made my way to the back. Grabbing two energy drinks, I met Caitlyn on the way back. Her face was white, tears running down silently. I closed my eyes as fresh tears ran down my own face. Making my way to the cashier, I added several boxes of Kleenex to my pile. My nose was running again.

After Jacob paid for everything, I returned to the van and made my way to the back. I waited wearily until everyone got in, then I started the van and made my way back onto the freeway. I drove about 15 miles to a deserted turnout beside a lake. The air looked rosy in the late-afternoon light.

I stopped the van and made my way to the back where Paula was sitting with Emily's head on her lap. Emily was as white as a ghost. Amazingly, she was awake. She looked at me, her eyes filled with dull pain.

"Alyssa," she whispered.

I sat down next to her and held her hand. Jacob, Caitlyn, Risa, and DeAndre came to sit with her too. Risa kissed Emily's cheek and knelt next to her, laying her head on Emily's middle. Emily's other hand came to rest on Risa's head, her fingers in Risa's wavy hair.

"Is anyone else hurt, guys?" Emily asked.

"No, Em. We're all okay. We're just worried about you," I said.

"I know I've been infected," she said. She closed her eyes in anguish, fresh tears running down her cheek. "I'm scared."

"Don't worry, Em, we're here. We're all here," said Jacob.

"Emily, look into my eyes," I said quietly. She turned her head and looked into my face. Her expression was an amalgam of worry, terror, sadness and resignation. I looked deep into her eyes. "Emily, we are all here. We are your friends, and we love you. Here, feel my hand." I squeezed her hand slightly. "Feel the warmth of my hand. I am here and Jake is here, and DeAndre and Caitlyn and even Risa here," I said as Risa wiggled up and kissed Emily's cheek. I smiled as Emily's face relaxed a bit into a smile. "We are all here, we love you and we are not going to go anywhere. There are things happening that we cannot stop, but nothing can stop our friendship. Nothing can stop our love for you. Whatever happens. Whatever comes. We will stay with you."

We sat with Emily for more than an hour, talking quietly, rubbing her hand, and just being. We had all been friends for the year. We had that chance to say goodbye to her. She grew quieter and quieter until she fell completely silent. We all just sat there in the afternoon light as the shadows slowly lengthened. Her eyes had been closed for several minutes when she spoke.

"Jake," she said quietly. Jacob pulled close to her face, and reached his hand out to caress her check.

"Jake, you must do something for me, when the end comes," she said.

"Anything, Em," Jacob said.

Emily voice became a whisper. "I don't want to turn into a zombie. When the time comes, you know what to do. You know."

Jacob nodded, looking into Emily's eyes. His face was pale but resolute. They had been friends since grade school. He would honor her wishes. She closed her eyes again and seemed to lose consciousness.

Paula checked her pulse. "I think she's asleep now," she said quietly.

We all sat and waited. It took two more hours. Thankfully, Emily slept through most of it. As her temperature rose, her face became pink, then red. She was burning up, in the last stages of the plague that was transforming her. Killing her. When her temperature suddenly dropped, DeAndre, Jacob and Mike carried her outside and gently laid her on the grass. We all gathered and waited. In the end, she opened her eyes one last time and focused on us, and it was still her.

"Thank you. For being my friends, for being with me," she said as her eyes closed again. She seemed to lose consciousness again. Five minutes later, her temperature dropped again and her face went from red to greyish. Jacob went and loaded the shotgun. He returned just as she began to thrash about. Tears streamed down his face as he held the barrel to her forehead. She began thrashing more, and Mike and DeAndre held her down. I looked away, and sobbed. Ten seconds later, the blast of Jacob's father's shotgun echoed across the parking lot and Emily's thrashing stopped and she was still. Caitlyn and Risa began to cry. The rest of us were just silent.

I looked into the mountains, toward the setting sun. I could hear the trees in the evening breeze and the wind whistling softly through the mountain canyons. It sounded like the ocean. I closed my eyes and inhaled deeply. The air was clean, fresh and pure. Like Emily had been. I would forever associate clean mountain air with Emily's death.

Holly went back into the van and emerged with a pale yellow blanket. She draped it around Emily's body, and with our help, wrapped her completely in the soft, thick material. Then she took her bag out and withdrew a needle and some thread. She began to sew the blanket closed. When she finished, Jacob, DeAndre and Mike carried the body to the side of the grass and placed it under a huge pine tree. Risa placed small yellow mustard flowers on top.

"An angel entered heaven today," I said quietly, hugging Risa as she cried softly. We made our way back to the van. Getting in, I felt weary and saddened beyond belief. I slid into the driver's seat and just sat there for a few minutes as everyone got in and situated. My chest felt heavy. I was beyond tears and to a realm of deep sadness people rarely experience. I felt much older than 17. In the past 36 hours, we had experienced so much, my shoulders felt as if they were burdened with hundred-pound weights. I felt so sad and shocked and

I felt I would never be the same. None of us would be. A dry sob suddenly issued forth from my lungs, and I reached for a Kleenex and blew my nose.

I was tired and weary and saddened to the point of shock. But I had to pull myself together. I didn't want anyone else to end up like Emily. Making a decision, I turned to Jacob and the others.

"I don't think we should drive into Los Angeles tonight. Something tells me it would a living nightmare. DeAndre, check the iPad and Twitter. Look up Los Angeles, zombie and plague hashtags. Meanwhile, I'm making an executive decision. We will sleep here for the night. It's quiet, deserted and peaceful. Spending the night here will give us the rest we're going to need tomorrow. That okay with everyone?"

They all nodded wearily.

"I think that's a good decision. I've been worrying about L.A. too, but I didn't want to say anything," said Jacob. "They took the evacuees there, and we can find them in the morning." I nodded and went to grab a blanket and a pillow from the back. Everyone else did the same, and we all got comfortable in our little van. Risa cuddled with the Scottie dog, which she had decided to name Blackie. Scooter lay across her feet.

We ended up spending an hour talking about Emily and reminiscing. Remembering her jokes during the Christmas play rehearsals and her goofy costume last Halloween.

"I never told anyone, and I don't think she did either, but last spring dance, I stole a kiss from her under the gym awning," confessed Jacob, smiling with tears in his eyes. "She told me she didn't feel ready for a boyfriend, but that I was a sweet guy."

I smiled, not the least bit jealous, which surprised me. Looking at Jacob, I saw he was looking into my face with an unreadable expression on his own face. "She was so sweet herself," I said, smiling as Jacob's face relaxed. "I think she was the best Alice I have ever seen," referring to her role in last years "Alice in Wonderland" that the team has performed. "Coach Turner worked so hard with her, but in the end the role just came naturally to her, she played it so smoothly. I really believed she *was* Alice, for just that hour."

DeAndre nodded. He had played the Cheshire cat in that production. "She was so easy to work with. She got along well with everyone. I will miss her so much." His voice caught in his throat.

I looked over at Risa and Holly, who were asleep against each other, Scooter and Blackie snuggled up against their feet. And towards the back, Ellie and Paula had conked out too. Mike was looking out the window. "Mike, you okay?" I said quietly, not wanting to wake the others.

He turned his head and I saw tears in the moonlight. "I'm fine," he said. "Just thinking." I nodded. The world had become unreal and uncertain. Sometimes the only way to cope was to step back from it. To think philosophically.

"You guys, I don't know what the coming days hold, but I really want to find out why this has happened, and if there's anything that can be done to reverse it" I tucked my head against my pillow and closed my eyes.

"Good night, Alyssa," Jacob said softly.

"G'night," I said as I drifted off into sleep.

Chapter Twelve

The night passed uneventfully, which was a nice change. It was barely morning when my eyes came open at the sound of movement beside me. It was Mike, getting a water bottle out of the front bags. Everyone else was still asleep, and dawn was breaking. The sun was still behind the row of mountains to our left as we talked in hushed tones.

"Did you sleep at all, Mike?" I asked.

"Yes. Jake was still up when I fell asleep. I just woke up about 5 minutes ago." He took a drink of water. "I'm heading out to the bathroom," he said, finishing the bottle and grabbing another. I nodded and stretched my back.

I reached for a towel and clean clothes and went outside to wash myself. I could hear the others begin to stir. I walked down to the edge of the lake in the cool air, feeling rested and alert. As I walked past where Emily's body lay, still and quiet under the giant tree, I felt a renewed determination to find out why my friends had to die. Emily didn't deserve what happened to her, and neither did Conner and Coach Turner.

I spent extra time in the water, washing myself thoroughly and scrubbing the grime off. I scrubbed until my skin was pink. Yesterday's events made me feel dirty and soiled. I felt I would never get clean, and I must have spent twenty minutes or more scrubbing myself. I was still trying to cleanse myself of the previous day's horror when Caitlyn and Risa came down with Holly, Paula, Ellie and the dogs. I just nodded to them and continued scrubbing. After finishing and dressing, I walked back from the lake feeling energized. Risa and Caitlyn were next to Emily. They had picked flowers and were putting them all around the blanket that covered her body. The dogs sniffed Emily's body, and then Blackie let out a whine and curled up next to Risa. Scooter sat on his haunches and let out a mournful howl, then fell silent. I walked over, kneeled beside her and made her a promise. I would find out why she had to die. I would find out what was going on and why it happened, and I would try to fix it if I could. I closed my eyes and whispered my goodbyes to Emily and then I got up and went to the van and got in.

In the van, I brushed my hair and put it in a ponytail, then grabbed some bread and jerky and munched on it until the others got in and closed the doors. I crossed my fingers that L.A. would be better in the daytime. It might have been wishful thinking, but we couldn't go back and we couldn't stay here. There was nowhere else to go, and our families were probably there … if they were still alive.

"Next stop: Los Angeles, where we will hopefully find our evacuated families. Sound good?" I asked. Looking over my shoulder I saw eight faces, all looking to me for answers. Even the three adults looked like they wanted guidance.

"Fresno, Bakersfield and the rest of the San Joaquin Valley were evacuated south. South to Los Angeles. I think we'll find answers there. I hope so. Is everyone okay and ready to go?" I asked.

"We're ready, Alyssa," Jake said. With a deep breath and a long drink out of my water bottle, I put the van in drive. Taking one last look at the small, sad bundle under the tree that had been Emily, I made her one last silent promise, wherever she was. If I could help it, I would do everything in my power not to let the plague take any more of us. I couldn't bear losing another friend.

The drive into Los Angeles took less than an hour. Just as we dropped down into the first of two sprawling valleys that held more than ten million people, sunlight broke through the morning haze and hit our vehicle like an angel's benediction.

"Alyssa, Twitter and CNN say the evacuees came to L.A. three days ago," Jake said. "Twitter has a few references on some being taken east, but mostly there's no word on any other mass movement. I did a search for the evacuation centers; they're all over the place."

"Okay, which ones are farthest north?" I figured evacuees from the north must have come down this same road and been settled somewhere in the San Fernando Valley.

"Well, there's school gymnasiums, hospitals, even office buildings where everyone was moved," Jacob said. "I'm not sure where we should look first. So many people being evac'ed, this may be chaos."

"They may have taken the injured to hospitals and the rest to large locations like school gyms or even parks," said Paula.

"Well, I need to stop at a gas station, maybe they'll know something there," I said.

About five minutes later, I saw a good turnoff that had several gas stations with minimarts. I pulled off the freeway and made my way into the am/pm parking lot and pulled up to a pump. Looking around, I saw a few people gassing up and some people in the store. Everything looked normal. I let out a long breath I hadn't realized I was holding. Putting the van in park, I turned off the engine and unbuckled my seatbelt.

"I'll get the gas going," Jacob said. He hopped out of the van but left his shotgun under the seat.

I got out to see what I could find out about the evacuations. I approached a man who was washing his windows while gas pumped into his car.

"Hey mister, would you know where they took everyone they evacuated from up north?" I asked.

"No, I don't know. I mean, I heard on the news they were taking some to area hospitals but that was two days ago. They might have moved them. You all from Bakersfield?"

"Some of us are from Bakersfield, some from Fresno. We had just got into town and had no idea what was going on. Is there any word about the cause of this emergency?"

"Not really but I heard there was some kind of infection and rioting to get away from it. They haven't told us much."

Paula stepped out of the van with Mike and Elsie. She approached us while Mike and Elsie went into the little store.

"Do they still have TV reports in L.A. about what's going on?" she asked. "Bakersfield went black yesterday afternoon."

"Yeah, there are some reports, but I don't think they know much. Just a bunch of 'stay in your houses' and 'don't panic' kind of stuff. I think they're worried about rioting in L.A. Do you know if this infection travels by air?"

"I believe it is transmitted by touch, maybe even by body fluids like saliva, but I'm not sure," Paula said.

I left them to talk and headed toward the minimart. As I walked, Risa walked up next to me and took my hand. I looked down at her and stopped to give her a hug. Then we walked into the store together. I went up to talk to the cashier, and Risa went to join Caitlyn in picking some snacks.

"Excuse me, we're from the San Joaquin Valley. Can you tell us where the rest of the evacuees were taken?" I asked.

"Oh, yeah," said the clerk, looking bored as she snapped her gum. "Um, I think they were taken down into the city. Most went to Griffith Park and the schools around there. That's where the police had set up their communications center."

"Thanks," I said, then turned to join the others. "Hey," I said, walking up to DeAndre and Caitlyn, "a lot of people were directed to the Griffith Park area, I think we should try there first."

"I was wondering about that park, it's huge. Makes sense they would gather them there," Jacob said, walking up to us.

I selected some snacks and several energy drinks and we all made our way back up to the clerk. She rang us up, gave a cautionary dismissal, and we left. As we crossed the parking lot, Mike came up to us.

"Hey guys, I want to thank you for helping me, but I think I'm going to move on. I've got some ideas about where to head to," he said.

"Okay, we're going to head on over to the Griffith Park area. You sure you don't want to tag along?" DeAndre said.

As we got to the van, Elsie poked her head out. "Can I borrow a phone? I'm going to call my niece in Pasadena, see if she can come get me."

"You can borrow mine," Caitlyn said, climbing in the van. I turned to Mike again.

"Mike, do you need to make a call or anything?" I asked.

"No, but on second thought, I think I will tag along with you guys until Griffith Park, if you don't mind," he said.

"Of course not," I said, getting into the van and popping open one of my energy drinks.

"Here are directions to the Park," Jacob said, handing me the iPad.

"Thanks," I said, glancing at it.

Everyone settled in their seats, and they were all talking about Griffith Park and the evacuations. I started the van and got back on the road.

"Man, I can't wait to get there. Finally, we're going to make some progress. I want to see my parents again, I hate this feeling of being separated from them," he said.

"Yeah, me too," I said, thinking about my mom and brother. I hoped they were okay. As I drove, I felt a renewed sense of energy. I was eager to find out what had happened. I felt a responsibility to Conner, Coach and Emily to discover all I could about the infection that had taken their lives. Everyone else seemed excited too, if the animated chatter behind me was any indication.

Chapter Thirteen

We made good time across the city; there was very little traffic. It was odd for Los Angeles, the city that practically invented traffic gridlock. I shivered involuntarily.

Within fifteen minutes, we were pulling up to Griffith Park. The police had cordoned the area off and were directing traffic around the park. As I pulled up to a stoplight where an officer was directing traffic, I rolled down the window and stuck my head out to ask him a question.

"Hi, we're looking for the people evacuated from Fresno and the San Joaquin Valley, do you know if they came here?"

"Go to the Observatory, that's where everyone was logged in. Here's a map," he said, waving us to the left entrance.

As we started pulling past him, I could hear the radio on his hip go off with a burst of static and then: *kkkkkkkk BACKUP! OFFICER DOWN! NEED BACKUP AT GREEK THEATRE! KKKKKKKKKKK* then the static took over and the mic went dead. The officer ran off toward the huddle of other police officers to our left, and the car behind us honked, so we continued down the road toward the observatory. I glanced at Jacob in the seat beside me, and he looked back at me, worried. That hadn't sounded good at all.

Four or five minutes later, we pulled up to the Griffith Observatory area. Police were swarming all over and the front of the observatory, which blazed with lights that made us shield our eyes even in full daylight. We parked and got out, locking the van and starting across the grass lawn. As we walked, we could see some commotion off to our right. About a dozen police officers were running toward an open-air theatre next to a structure of some kind. I couldn't see what was going on, but we heard faint yelling and then nothing.

"Oh, Jesus," I mumbled as we walked.

"Let's just get to the observatory," DeAndre said next to me.

"If that commotion is what I'm afraid it might be, this infection is spreading really fast. Faster than it should," Paula said behind me.

Risa came up to me on the right, wiggling between me and DeAndre and slipped her hand into mine. On my left, Jacob did the same. I glanced at him, but he continued walking and looking straight ahead, and he gave my hand a squeeze as we walked. My heart fluttered, and I felt a warm sensation in my chest.

"Will my daddy be here, Alyssa?" asked Risa.

"We hope so, Sweetie, but let's just see, okay? I hope my mom and brother are here, and Jacob hopes his mom is here. Everyone wants to be back with their families," I said, trudging on.

As we approached the observatory, we passed the statue of Griffith J. Griffith and I giggled suddenly.

"I'm sorry. It's just a silly sounding name," I said, smiling. Risa giggled then, and soon we were all laughing as we walked up the concrete walkway and to the large doors of the building. It was a welcomed release of all the pent-up tension that had been building up in us for days, and although it seemed misplaced considering what we had been through, we couldn't help ourselves. By the time we got to the doors, all nine of us were laughing so hard we were having trouble walking. Holly was clutching her big pregnant belly she was laughing so hard. I wiped the tears of laughter from my eyes as I mounted the stairs to the heavy front doors. Releasing Risa's hand, I pulled them open and we all walked in.

We entered the observatory and closed the doors behind us and stood there taking everything in. It was carefully controlled chaos. People milled about everywhere, and officials tried to take care of them, but there were too many people. Through a doorway on our right, we could see some kind of triage. Pallets lay side by side with people on them. Some injured people were sitting against the wall. Resources were stretched beyond their limits.

On our left, we saw a large room that had been set up with bunk beds. A lot of children and a few adults occupied this room, attended by people in military uniforms. Up ahead was an area set aside for dispensing food, and a line of several dozen people snaking back away from a couple of tables.

As we watched, we heard a man in uniform call out: "The next 50 people, over here!" A group moved off with him. A woman in uniform stood nearby. She seemed to be a guard, and was as likely a candidate as anyone to answer our questions.

"Excuse me," I said, approaching her slowly with my hand outstretched and a smile on my face, "we are looking for our families. They were evac'ed from Fresno and Bakersfield. Can you help us?"

"Go to the rear of the auditorium on your left and see the man at the desk under the purple banner," she said tersely. "All new arrivals went through that checkpoint. But most of them are being moved to Arizona, that's what the buses are loading for."

"Thank you," I said as she turned to help another person. I

motioned to the rest of my group and made my way through the auditorium and to the desk she had indicated. We had to weave our way in and out of groups of people to get there, people just seemed to be waiting for something. I searched the faces as we walked, but I didn't see my family or anyone else I recognized. Some of the faces looked worried and some badly frightened. Others looked bored and sleepy. There were more children than adults, which made me wonder if they had evacuated the schools down here without waiting for the parents. I hoped not. That would make it hard for the parents and kids to find each other. I knew what that felt like. But maybe the officials had had no choice.

I pushed my way through the last group and found myself at the information desk, the others gathered behind me.

"Hello," I said to get the man's attention.

"Just a moment," he replied, turning to the computer in front of him and walking several yards to the side to speak with another official. After several minutes he returned and addressed us.

"Can I help you?" he said.

"Yes. Thank you. We're from Fresno and Bakersfield, and we are looking for our families who were evacuated a day or so before us. Do you have a list of people who were moved here from up north?" I asked.

"Uh, well, I do have a partial list, but we've already begun moving most of the folks from the northern valley and coast. The buses started this morning, and the last of them are loading this afternoon. What are their names?" he said as he began to type.

We told him the names of each of our family members, and he checked his database. It turned out that most of our families had been routed to Arizona and were likely already on their way there.

"You can try to check the people waiting to get on the last busses, but they've most likely already left," he finished. I nodded and moved off to a corner with my friends.

"Guys, I still want to try and check the rest of the people they're moving, okay? You never know, and I would hate to miss them if they're here," I said.

"I don't have any family, I lived alone," said Paula. "I'm going to check with their medics and see if they could use another pair of hands. Mike, you want to come with?"

"I guess so," Mike answered, "but first let me go with Alyssa and check if anyone I know is here."

Paula moved off to the triage area through the center room. Meanwhile, we made our way through the center area and toward the rear, where the people loading onto buses had gone through.

We spent about an hour wandering through the crowd of about two thousand people waiting to be moved to Arizona, looking for our families, but with no luck. Moving back through the building, Jacob and DeAndre stopped in the bathroom. Waiting for them, Caitlyn, Holly and I stood with Risa and talked.

"Maybe it would be good to check the medic center, in case someone's in there," Caitlyn said.

"I was hoping to avoid that, but you're right, it would be stupid not to check it. Risa, want to get something to eat?" I said as DeAndre stepped out of the bathroom with Jacob following. Risa nodded tiredly, and I took her hand and turned to nod at everyone. We all went to the food counter.

Sitting at a table we had found, munching on sandwiches and apples, I turned to Jacob.

"Looks like we may be heading to Arizona next. How's your

money holding up?" I said.

"Still have plenty left. Do you think we should find some place to sleep here overnight before we drive east? I'm so tired," he said wearily.

"I don't know if we can, because of all the people here from the evacuations, but I wouldn't mind sleeping in a real bed," I said, smiling. He smiled back at me and put his hand on mine where it sat on the table. I blushed and took his hand in mine.

We continued eating and people-watching. There was so much to look at in the observatory, and none of it really had anything to do with the building. It was the people. All different walks of life were represented. People dressed in black and heavily tattooed, and people in business suits and families with small, tired children. They were all thrown together in this crisis. The infection had spread to every social strata: no one had been left untouched. And something told me that things were going to get much, much worse before they ever got better. Wearily, I stood and threw the paper from my sandwich into the nearby trash can.

Chapter Fourteen

"I'm going to go check out the medics' room and see if anyone I know is there," I said. "Who's coming with me?"

Risa jumped up quickly, energized by her ten minutes of rest and the peanut butter and jelly sandwich I had gotten her, grabbed my hand, and smiled up at me, ready for anything. I smiled back down at her and felt someone take my other hand. It was Jacob. I looked into his eyes and smiled. He smiled back, and leaned forward.

"Lead the way, Alyssa," he said, and gave me a light kiss on the cheek. It felt wonderful. Smiling, I began walking toward the medic room. The others, having nowhere else to go and no one else leading them, followed us. We made our way through the crowd and stopped just inside the entrance to the large room where every injured person in L.A. seemed to be gathered.

Some of the injuries looked "normal" – like it had happened during a fall or when a crowd had panicked and stampeded. Others looked far worse. Some had head or limbs wrapped; others were unconscious. And some of them were very, very pale – nearly grey. My eyes widened, and I swallowed nervously. Turning to the others, I saw similar looks of worry on their faces. They had noticed it, too.

"All right guys, be on alert," I said. "We may have to run at any moment. You know what I'm talking about."

They all nodded silently.

We slowly walked down the aisle, looking back and forth to see if we recognized anyone. We passed one woman who was grey and thrashing. They had tied her to the bed. She pulled at her restraints as several nurses tried to calm her. I wondered if the ties would hold. I prayed they would but watched her carefully as we passed, in case they didn't. I wasn't sure, but it seemed as if the infection gave the victims extra strength. Or maybe it numbed their brains, overriding the instinct that tells us to stop pulling/pushing/lifting when our limbs seem about ready to break. This might be turned off in the plague victims. Which would be terrible for the rest of us. They seemed so crazed they would stop at nothing to break free and attack, even if it meant injuring themselves in the process.

We passed a lot of kids who had been injured in crowd panics. They were a sad sight, but I was glad they hadn't been infected. Then Paula came up to us, holding a list several pages long in her hand.

"This is a partial list of patients that were so bad off they were transferred to Cedars Sinai Medical Center," she said, handing us the sheaf of papers. We clustered together as Jacob leafed through the pages. I was terrified my mom or brother would be on the list, but at the same time I would finally know where they were. I didn't know what to hope for, but I looked eagerly over Jacob's shoulder at the names on each page.

Maybe it was a blessing that no one we knew was on the list. I hoped they were safely in Arizona by now. Unexpectedly, I felt tears well up in my eyes. Jacob looked at me with concern. I just smiled a watery smile up at him through my unshed tears. It was just so emotional, it was exhausting. He looked at me silently for a moment and then put his arms around me in a hug, handing the list over to Mike so the others could finish checking.

I put my head on Jacob's shoulder and my arms loosely around his waist and closed my eyes. We stood there like that for a long time. After a minute, Risa came up behind me and put her arms around me, and then Caitlyn and DeAndre came and joined our hug, and we all just held each other, relieved that our families had not been on the injured list, tired from the days-long ordeal we were going through.

Suddenly, behind me about 20 feet away, the woman who had been tied to the bed began growling in a low, menacing tone and thrashing so hard against her restraints that her bed came off the floor repeatedly. Several orderlies and nurses were trying to settle her down, and a doctor came running with a syringe that I hoped contained some kind of sedative.

"AHHHHH!!!!" screamed one of the nurses and backed up, clutching his bleeding forearm. He had been bitten. As we watched, the crazed woman got one of her legs free and flipped her bed over. She was now thrashing about on the floor and had gotten partially free.

"Let's get out of here, guys," I said as I moved down the aisle. The other patients that were conscious all looked toward the commotion with fear in their eyes. They knew what could happen. I didn't know if these doctors and nurses had been briefed on what the victims of this plague could do. If they had been, I didn't think they would be that close to the thrashing woman, who was now turning dark grey and nearly free of her restraints. I wasn't even sure any sedative would work. The plague victims-turned-zombies seemed almost super-human. I wasn't sure any medicine would affect them. Nothing but brute force seemed to have any impact.

I hustled us towards the door at the other end of the large room. We were nearly there when we heard a scream from behind us, and I turned involuntarily to see the man on the bed next to the thrashing woman screaming as she clawed and bit him. She had gotten free, and the three nurses and two orderlies had run. The doctor was still trying to give her the shot, but she was wild, thrashing and kicking.

The bedridden man continued to scream, and she continued to fight with him. Then the doctor tried to grab her with both arms, to get her away from the other patient, and she turned on him and bit him in the face. As he screamed, blood poured down his neck and she chewed on his cheek and wrapped her hands around his neck to hold on.

I shuddered and turned around and began running. Getting to the doorway, I sneaked another peek over my shoulder and saw the doctor go down, the zombie on top of him, still chewing. God, I thought, this place is going mad. Just as I turned to go through the door, it opened from the other side.

"OH MY GOD, THEY'RE OUTSIDE, AT THE THEATRE!! THEY'RE COMING THIS WAY!" screamed a man as he bolted into the medic room. We were pushed aside in his panic, and Risa fell. DeAndre reached down and picked her up and looked at me. "Which way?" he asked.

I made a quick decision and opened the door and looked out. Bad, very bad. At least five zombies were loping toward the observatory door. They looked to be coming from the theatre, just as the man had said. I quickly looked beyond them and saw at least a dozen bodies on the grass, and police officers running toward the theatre. If they were running *toward* the theatre, when the zombies were running *away* from it, what on earth worse was at the theatre, I wondered? What could be worse?

Retreating back into the sick room, I turned to the others, "We need to bolt this door somehow, they're coming fast."

Mike shut the door and locked it, and we faced the inner room. The zombie was still on the ground with the doctor, who was still screaming. I looked around. No one else seemed to have turned, but several looked close. There was only the other door out of the room. Our only escape route. I nodded at DeAndre with Risa and Jacob and Caitlyn and Holly.

"Follow me," I said. I moved slowly, trying not to draw the zombie's attention. At first it seemed to be working, she was concentrating on her victim on the ground and had her back turned to us. We were almost passed her when, all of a sudden, she noticed us. Blood dripped from her mouth as she focused on us and let out an angry growl.

"Come on!" I said and began sprinting toward the door. DeAndre threw Risa over his shoulder and followed. The others were fast on our heels. I looked over my shoulder as I ran, just in time to see Ellie fall and cry out in pain. Mike grabbed her and kept moving. Ellie clutched her arm and stumbled with him. Paula had joined us again and ran to help Ellie. I looked past them to the zombie.

The zombie had started to get up to follow us, but as she stumbled over the bleeding doctor on the floor, he grabbed her ankle and held on with both hands. As I watched, his eyes met ours and he yelled, "Run!"

Enraged by his actions, the zombie turned back to him and fell on him again, growling madly. We heard him scream again. He had sacrificed himself to save us.

I ran through the door we had used to enter the room and, when the others were through, I closed it firmly and turned to the outer room. Several security guards were racing toward us to help. They opened the door and ran into the room, guns drawn. We put some distance between us and that door, in case they were unable to get a handle on things.

Several shots rang out, and we could hear someone yelling orders. More officers were moving quickly into the area. I grabbed the others, and we ran to the far doors that had led to the buses that were leaving for Arizona. The crowded room was in a panic, everyone had heard what was happening in the medic room. I grabbed Jacob's hand and he grabbed Caitlyn's. With my other hand I grabbed DeAndre's shirt as he carried Risa. The others linked hands as well. We formed a chain and banded together closely and made our way around the edge of the panicked crowd toward the outside door. It was close to the entry we had first come through, so I hoped that the busses were near our van.

As we made our way around the panicked crowd, I turned to the others. "Stay on the edge," I told them. "Do not get pulled into the crowd." Everyone nodded and followed me through the room and to the door. We were about 25 feet from the exit when I felt the crowd surge against us. The medic room doors had opened, and two grey-faced zombies had appeared in the doorway. They must have come through the far door or had turned just after the first woman. Either way, the sight and sound of this new threat threw the crowd into a frenzy. They were mad to get away from the zombies. People started screaming and pushing against us, trying to get to the door along with us. A bottleneck formed, and the people began to claw at one another, trying to get out. Holly cried out and fell against me. Then she went down, clutching her arm. I grabbed her and got her back on her feet. She held her pregnant belly and looked into my eyes. Her face was white with fear. Blood dripped from a deep cut on her arm where someone had clawed her. We hurriedly scrambled to the side, trying to escape the panicked crowd.

This was madness, I thought. Worse than a fire at a theatre. We were against a wall ten feet from the door, but there were several hundred people pushed up against it and against us, all frantic and growing more violent by the second. When some of them began to climb over the others, trampling them, I knew we needed to get out of there. I frantically searched above our heads, trying to see another way out.

At the far end of the room, near the medic doors and the

zombies, a wide staircase curled up to the second floor, which looked like an open atrium and walkway. I glanced at the zombies near the far doorway. They were growling and beginning to advance toward the crowd pressed against our end of the room. There was maybe forty feet of space between the edge of the crowd and the zombies. I backed up and began to make my way around the crowd, hugging the wall and trying as hard as I could to avoid attracting the zombies' attention. Jacob, DeAndre with Risa, Holly and Caitlyn began to follow my lead.

Ellie saw what we were doing and panicked. She screamed and began clawing her way through the crowd to get to the outside door. One man began to claw back at her, trying to stay on top of the people he had clawed through already. Ellie screamed as she went down and the crowd swallowed her. It happened in just a few seconds. The people surged toward the door, and the man, along with several dozen others, turned to continue climbing on top of the screaming people as Ellie's screams became muffled and weaker.

"Oh my God!" Mike exclaimed as he began trying to dig through the crowd to help her. We all came and tried to get to her, Jacob and Mike in the front, grabbing people and shoving them aside. This seemed to panic the crowd further, and they began fighting back. Within minutes, a dozen people were punching and fighting Mike, Jacob and the rest of us as we tried to get to Ellie. We fell back several times, overwhelmed. Paula fell into the crowd once, and Jacob grabbed her leg and pulled her out, but the minute she had been under the trampling feet and pounding fists had been enough. As she was pulled out of there, we saw her face had been bloodied and her arm hung limp. She was in a daze. We pulled her to the side and away from the crowd.

Mike stood back up and wanted to jump into the crowd again to rescue Ellie, but I held his arm. "Mike, it's no use. They're going to trample you, too if you jump back in there."

He hung his head, tears in his eyes.

"She's my mom's age. I have to try," he said. I nodded. He jumped back into the crowd and tried to weave around the worst offenders who were still trying to climb over the others. Jacob went with him, and DeAndre joined him after putting Risa gently down beside Paula, who was groaning.

I turned back to the doctor. Looking her over, it seemed that her head had been trampled on and her arm had been caught underneath her as she fell. Holly sat on the floor and held Paula's head in her lap. Paula groaned and opened her eyes.

"How're you feeling?" I asked, trying to wipe some of the blood off her face with a napkin that had been dropped nearby.

Groaning in pain, she seemed halfway delirious. Holly smoothed her hair away from her bloody face, but the back of her head was bleeding, too.

"Bastards," Paula whispered, then fell unconscious. Her head must have gotten knocked around. Risa and Caitlyn crouched down with them as I got up to look for help. Looking around, I could no longer see Mike, Jacob or DeAndre at all. God, I hoped they were okay. I looked for anyone who could help us. But everyone, including nurses, orderlies and some security guards who had panicked, were in the midst of the stampeding crowd that was trying frantically to get out the door. I looked beyond them to the far door to the medic room and saw that the zombies had advanced farther and were attacking the people on the edge of the crowd. I turned back to Paula and the others.

"I'm going to get some water to clean her head up," I said to Holly, Caitlyn and Risa. "Can you hold the fort for a second?" They nodded and, keeping a close eye on the crowd and zombies, I hurriedly walked toward the tables we had eaten lunch at not an hour before. I found a glass of water and some discarded napkins and, grabbing both, I made my way back to the injured doctor. Kneeling down, I wetted the napkins and began to clean the blood off her face. It looked like just superficial wounds for the most part, except for the back of her head. She was out cold. She had probably fallen and cracked her skull; there was a mass of blood there. Paula's dress was nearly soaked. I wiped up her face, and she groaned as I worked. Regaining consciousness, she was able to sip a bit of the water I had.

"Oh, my head!" she groaned.

"I know, just try to take it easy. You've banged your head pretty bad, and I think your arm has been injured, too," I said as I looked down at her arm.

Paula blinked her eyes, trying to wake up fully. After a few moments, she came to completely and sat up more on her own. I handed the glass of water to Caitlyn and stood up. Turning toward the crowd again, my eyes searched for the guys. I saw Jacob backing out of the crowd pulling Ellie's limp body behind him. He had to pushed back and fight the mob as he moved backward. DeAndre followed, helping Mike. He halfway carried him, Mike's left leg seemed to be collapsed under him, and his head was bleeding badly.

I grimaced and closed my eyes tight for a moment, then opened them again and looked down at Ellie. She wasn't moving. Jacob pulled her to the side and kneeled next to her, feeling for a pulse at her neck. After a minute he raised his head and our eyes met. He shook his head quietly. I felt tears spring to my eyes as I dropped them to Ellie's still form. It had all happened so fast, I couldn't believe it. I heard Mike groan behind me, and I turned to him and DeAndre. Mike was in bad shape. It looked like his jaw was broken and one eye was swollen shut. His left leg was folded beneath him at an odd angle.

"What happened?" I asked.

DeAndre just shook his head. "They're crazed. He was in front of them and they turned on him. One huge guy got in several punches to his face before he stopped, and then he fell, and three other guys began to climb on top of him and stomped his leg at the knee," he finished.

I looked down at Mike's leg, feeling it. He winced and grabbed at the leg as I felt his knee.

"I'm going to straighten it out, Mike, okay?" I said. He nodded, his face contorted in pain. As I gently pulled his foot over, straightening his leg out, he cried out. His face went white and he broke out in a sweat. He seemed close to passing out from the pain. Mike's leg needed to be set; he needed medical help now, and Paula was in no condition to help. I looked around again at the chaos in the room and shook my head. No help was in sight. None.

We all huddled together like that as the crazed mob not fifteen feet away from us continued to scramble to get through the doorway and away from the zombies clawing at their edge. A few made it out, but most of the doorway was stopped up with bodies piled three or four deep. They had been trampled, and many of them were unconscious – or worse. As I looked, I heard more faint screaming coming from the medic room. I looked everywhere for assistance. The police were outside or in the medic room battling zombies in there. The security guards who were left had joined the nurses, orderlies and the hundreds of civilians in stampeding the doors. I looked back at the others and made a decision.

Chapter Fifteen

"We have to get out of here. This isn't safe," I said. "Grab Mike and Paula, and let's try and get out of here. Come on."

Caitlyn glanced over at Ellie. "What about her?" she asked.

I just shook my head. "No," Caitlyn said in a whisper, closing her eyes. Holly began to cry softly. I shook my head. This was madness. I grabbed Paula around the middle and helped her to her feet. Jacob and DeAndre both got Mike to his feet. Caitlyn shuddered and Holly and Risa sniffled as we started moving again, making our way toward the staircase. We hugged the wall and tried to stay as far away as we could from the zombies attacking the crowd. Luckily for us, the people at the edge being attacked were fighting back, and the zombies' attention was fully engaged in subduing their prey. We made it to the edge of the staircase and began to climb, still staying as far away as possible from the chaos near the exit. At the top of the staircase, we saw the second floor led to an outside balcony and an elevator. No one down on the first floor seemed to realize there was another way out, but that could change at any moment. "Let's go outside on the balcony, guys," I said. Everyone went through the doors, and they closed behind us.

I whispered to Jacob, "If those people in there knew this elevator was here, they'd kill us to get to it."

He nodded grimly.

When the doors closed, the near-deafening sound of the mob and the zombies was replaced by near silence. I stopped for a moment to catch my breath. Holding Paula up wasn't easy. After a few minutes, I looked at the others and then turned to the elevators. I shifted Paula and reached out to press the call button for the elevator.

I held my breath. It seemed to take an eternity for the elevator to arrive, but the doors slid open without a problem. Thankfully, the elevator was empty.

"That was madness, goddammit," Jacob said angrily as the elevator began to descend. "Those people are insane! They just attacked us!"

"What happened to Ellie?" asked Risa.

"Sweetie, I can't say, I just can't," I answered. I straightened up as the elevator came to a halt. The doors slid open and we peered out. The area looked quiet, no zombies or crazed people nearby, so we slowly made our way around the side of the building. Mike grimaced at the pain but was able to stumble along with help. We went around the long way, to avoid the theatre side of the Observatory and the stampeded doorway. Coming around to the front of the building, I peered out and scanned the area. I could hear the people trying to get through the doorway, but what concerned me more were the sounds coming from beyond them from around the second corner that led to the theatre grounds. No screaming, but a low rumbling of growls and moans. Looking beyond the front grassy area to the parking lot, I saw our van, parked and waiting. A tantalizing sight. The walkway from the front of the building to the parking lot was a long and completely open expanse. Open to view from the front door where they were rioting. Open to view from the theatre side, where I believed the zombies were overtaking the area.

I looked back at our ragtag group. Mike and Paula were being helped along. Holly was pregnant. Risa looked up at me solemnly. She had been watching me assess the situation.

"We can make it, Alyssa. We can run fast," she said seriously. I studied her young face for a minute. She looked sure of herself. Determined. Resolute. Looking into the others' faces I saw them looking back at me. We had lost Ellie back in that building. We had almost lost Paula and Mike too. But they looked back at me and their faces were serious and set. I nodded. We would run for it.

I estimated the distance at about 100 yards. The length of a football field. Glancing back at my people, I gave them a short nod and said, "Okay. Let's do this." Turning back, I held Risa's hand and began sprinting to the van. Behind me, Caitlyn helped Paula run and DeAndre and Jacob half carried Mike along. Holly ran beside us, clutching her large, pregnant belly.

As we rounded the front corner and came within sight of the mobbed entry, a new group of rioters broke free from the doorway and began running too. Quite a few of them were running in our direction. Then, as the theatre grounds came into full view, the growling from that area grew louder. I glanced over as I ran and gasped. No fewer than a dozen zombies were loping toward us, encouraged by the rioters, who were screaming in the doorway. I took a breath and ran faster. Behind me, I heard Caitlyn pant, "Alyssa, help us!"

Paula was half stumbling, so I ran back and grabbed her other side while Risa got behind and pushed her toward the van. A moment later, we were all running again. Jacob and DeAndre had gotten about ten feet ahead of us. Beside us, Holly panted and ran as fast as she could at eight-plus months pregnant. As I ran, I looked back and to the side again. Most of the zombies from the theatre area had run at the riot crowd, but some had broken away to pursue the people making a dash for the parking lot with us. They were slightly to the side of us though, between us and the zombies. We ran on, we were more than halfway there.

Paula groaned and stumbled again. Her head wound was causing her to slip in and out of consciousness. I heard Caitlyn moan in fright, and we practically lifted Paula off her feet as we stumbled toward the safety of our van. I heard a growl closer behind us, and I looked back to see two of the zombies had decided to come after us. Risa ran around Paula and took off toward Jacob, DeAndre and Mike, who were closing in on the van. That little girl could run! I glanced back at Holly, who was panting hard and holding her belly as if it hurt her.

"Hey, you okay?" I asked as I ran along. Holly just gave me a scared look and kept loping. Looking ahead, I saw that we were about 75 feet from the parking lot. Behind us though, the zombies were gaining ground. One of them, who looked like a businessman in a dark suit with a blue tie, was nearly upon us. The look in his eyes was terrifying. His face was a dark grey, and his eyes were milky. Dark blood, almost black, dripped from his head, down the side of his face, and down his arm. He loped behind us in a kind of sideways gait that was keeping pace with us, about 15 feet behind Holly.

Jacob and DeAndre had made it to the van. They had unlocked it and were getting Mike into it. Risa ran up to them and scampered into the back of the van like a terrified kitten. Jacob glanced back at us and gasped. Then he reached into the van. I groaned. Why couldn't he come help us? Paula was hard to move. When he emerged from the van with his father's shotgun and began running back to us, I suddenly understood why. Caitlyn saw what was happening too and, straining to get a better hold on Paula, began to run even faster. We were nearly there when Jacob caught up to us ... and ran past us. Gasping in surprise, I looked back as I ran and saw that Holly had stumbled and the zombie was nearly on her.

"Go help them, we can get Paula into the van," Caitlyn said as we reached the vehicle. DeAndre had come back out and was helping her with Paula. I turned and dashed back to Holly and Jacob. Just as Jacob reached her, Holly stood back up and took two steps toward us, but it was too late. The zombie leapt as she tried to escape and landed half on her, arms reaching to her waist and pulling her to the ground again. She landed hard on her belly and cried out.

Just as the zombie was grasping at her and growling, trying to bite her, Jacob caught up to them and leveled his shotgun at the zombie's head.

He fired.

The resulting blast blew half the zombie's head away, splattering both Holly and Jacob with blood, brains and bits of dark grey flesh. The grotesque figure in the dark suit and blue tie fell backward and lay partially on top of Holly. Jacob leaned down to grab her arm, to drag her out from under the disgusting mess. I grabbed her around the waist, and we pulled her out, but just then we heard more growling.

It was coming from just a few feet away – a second zombie was nearly upon us.

"Jesus!" Jacob exclaimed, straightening up and cocking the shotgun once again. As the zombie ran up to us, Jacob let loose another round, catching the zombie in the midsection. The creature fell to the ground moaning. We got Holly to her feet and stumbled to the van. Somehow, the zombie picked itself up and began hobbling toward us. I looked back, disbelieving.

"I shoulda hit it in the head, it's the only thing that seems to stop them," Jacob mumbled as we piled into the van and slid the door shut. As I settled into the driver's seat, the zombie fell against the side window of the door we had just closed. It banged the window hard with its fists, making a hollow sound on the inside.

"Here!" Jacob yelled as he tossed me the keys. I caught them and fumbled to put them into the ignition. Why didn't these things go smoothly in an emergency? I finally got the key in and started up the van. As the engine rumbled to life, I quickly threw it in gear. I wanted to get the hell out of here fast. Glancing back, I began to reverse out of the parking lot.

All of a sudden, fists pounded against my driver's side window. Three other zombies had joined the one pounding the other window and were now trying to break through mine. One grabbed at the side windows and another held tight to the door handle, pounding hard at the window, inches from my face.

"Oh, hell no!" I exclaimed, accelerating backward and screeching out of the parking lot, burning rubber. Two of the zombies fell to the ground, and a third tried to grab hold of the side-view mirror. I dragged it along for a few dozen yards before it fell off to the side. I sped down the road so fast the van wobbled from side to side as I maneuvered down the street. I had had enough. Every one of that stampeding crowd could fall to the zombies as far as I was concerned. Ellie hadn't deserved to get trampled to death, and Mike and Paula hadn't deserved to be injured by a crazed mob. I drove fast back the way we had come, finding the freeway in minutes. I turned onto the southbound entrance and accelerated down the road, wiping the tears from my eyes.

Chapter Sixteen

I brought the car quickly up to freeway speed, took a shuddering breath and reached for my water.

What an ordeal.

"Alyssa," Jacob said quietly, "We have a problem."

Slowing down a little, I glanced back at him, a foreboding feeling gathering in my gut. "What's going on?" I asked.

Jacob came up to the front and settled into the seat beside me. "Keep going," he said. "We need to get out of the city."

I glanced over at him. He almost seemed afraid to tell me whatever it was he had to say. It must be bad, I thought.

I waited.

"It's Holly."

My stomach fell. Her baby! I waited in silence for Jacob to continue.

"She had the cut from the mob back at the Observatory, and when she fell on the grass, she was scraped up pretty bad on her elbow," he said.

"Yes? Is she okay now?" I said, not understanding.

Jacob sighed and looked down. Swallowing hard, he continued.

"The zombie that jumped her was bleeding a lot and was covered in fluids. It got all over her when the creature was on her. Then I shot it and further sprayed her with … fluids from it," he said. "Her skin and clothes were soaked with that crud. Its blackish blood was all over her cut."

It was a moment before I realized what he was trying to say. Then it dawned on me: Holly might be infected.

Swallowing hard, I nodded. "Okay. Well, let's see," I couldn't think.

Jacob said, "I think the first order of business is to get out of the city. We have no idea which areas are safe, so we should assume all areas are compromised. I say we drive south or east and get as far from L.A. as possible."

I nodded. "Are you sure she's infected? Try and clean her off. There are water bottles in the back. Get her into dry clothes and just throw the dirty stuff out the window. Try to clean that cut. It's a small chance, but maybe she'll be okay."

"If the cut didn't go through all the layers of skin, she may have a chance," DeAndre said, coming up to the front. "The cut is looking good, I cleaned and bandaged it. I personally don't think she's infected."

I turned and looked toward the back of the van and saw Holly sitting up and talking with Caitlyn. She seemed fine and normal. I breathed a sigh of relief.

"Let's hope you're right, D," I sighed, suddenly exhausted. "Not only for her sake, but for her baby's," I finished.

Nodding, DeAndre moved back to the rear seat. Jacob glanced at me and said, "You okay to drive?"

"I think so. Although I sure could use about three days of sleep," I said, grimacing. I could feel the exhaustion coming in waves, washing over my entire body, but I tamped down the feeling, determined not to slow down until we were safe.

"Someone get on the iPad and find me a hospital, either going toward San Diego or Phoenix," I said. "I'm putting a couple hundred miles between us and L.A." Preferably one not flooded by zombies, I added in my head. I drove south on I-5 and tried to think about something other than Holly's baby. On the one hand, I trusted DeAndre's judgment about her wound. On the other, I had a very bad feeling about the situation.

Jacob reached for his tablet and lifted the black rectangle out of the side panel where he had stuck it earlier. "I need to plug it in anyway," he said. He pulled the car adaptor out of the glove compartment, plugged everything in and got to work. Glancing at me with sad eyes, he said, "This'll keep me busy, hopefully get my mind off the crap situation we just got out of." He smiled grimly and lowered his eyes again to the tablet. After a few minutes, he looked up.

"I think we should take the 10 freeway out to Arizona. We don't know the situation in San Diego, and they diverted everyone east. Mike, Paula, and Holly will be okay for a few more hours. Their bleeding is stopped and none of them is in shock.

I nodded tiredly and began to look for the I-10 turnoff from I-5 southbound. I felt my body calming down as I drove. It had been flooded with adrenaline from the freakish afternoon we had just had, but now as I became calmer, I felt myself becoming very drowsy. With a sigh, I realized I hadn't slept in 48 hours. I began to fantasize about lying down in a soft bed and falling asleep.

"HEY!!" Jacob said loudly as he grabbed the wheel. I had dozed off and the van had veered toward the side of the road.

"Oh my God, I'm sorry," I mumbled. Bringing the van to a stop at the side of the road, I put it in park and turned to the others. "Who's good to drive?" I asked.

"Never mind them. I can drive, Alyssa," Jacob said as I moved to the side seat. He slid behind the driver's wheel and handed me the iPad. "You should try to sleep. It'll be at least six hours before we get to Phoenix."

Nodding, I buckled myself in and looked back to the others; most of them were in various states of slumber. We were all so exhausted. Glancing down at the iPad, I thought about doing research on our situation and the West Coast retreat to Arizona, but my eyes were burning and my head felt so fuzzy. All of a sudden I was so tired I couldn't keep my eyes open. I had no more energy to fight it, and I fell soundly asleep.

Chapter Seventeen

"Wake up, Alyssa," Jacob said as he gently shook me awake. I woke up and saw we had pulled off the freeway and were in a hospital parking lot. The others were gathering Paula and Mike together and exiting the van. Holly jumped down onto the asphalt and seemed fine, talking with Caitlyn and helping Risa down. The sun was just setting against the desert landscape.

"How long did I sleep?" I asked, still groggy.

"About two hours, give or take. It's about 7:30," Jacob said. "I decided to stop here in Indio at Kennedy Memorial. We need Paula, Mike and Holly checked out. Paula passed out again about an hour ago, and Mike's leg is broken or dislocated or something, he says he can't stand the pain. And I want Holly's arm checked out. She says it's not bothering her, but...." His voice trailed off.

I nodded and blinked the sleepiness out of my eyes. Even two hours of sleep had refreshed me, I decided, jumping down out of the van. Scooter and Blackie whined and begged to come with us, but after a few minutes on some nearby grass, we put them back in the van. We had enough on our hands just taking care of Paula, Mike and Holly.

"Holly, how are you feeling?" I asked. I saw that she had cleaned herself up nicely, and had on new jeans and a fresh t-shirt.

"I'm feeling fine. My arm isn't even sore," she said, smiling.

I hugged her and swallowed back tears of relief. "I'm so glad. How is Baby doing?" I asked.

Holly looked down at her protruding belly and patted it gently. "I think he's doing great. While I dozed, he was moving a lot. I'm about three weeks from my due date, so I'm going to have them check everything here, but I'm sure he's just fine."

I reached over and tousled Risa's hair. "And how're you holding up, Sweetie?"

"Pretty good, but I'm hungry," Risa answered, looking up at me.

"Well, then. Let's see what kind of grub we can rustle up for you at this joint," I said. I held on to Paula's right arm, and Caitlyn took her left. Holly took Risa's hand in hers, and we looked back at the guys.

"Mike's leg's swollen up pretty bad, I'm going to get them to come out here with a stretcher for him," DeAndre said.

"I'll stay with him, you ladies go on ahead. We'll meet you inside" Jacob said.

Nodding, we turned back toward the Emergency Room entrance and slowly made our way into the waiting room. Risa and I sat with Paula as Caitlyn and Holly went up to talk to a nurse. I saw DeAndre come in and do the same, then head back out, followed by two nurses with a stretcher for Mike. Looking back into the room, I spied several vending machines in the corner.

"Risa, look: there are some snacks. Here," I said, handing her a few dollars, "go and bring me back something and get yourself a treat, too."

"What kind of snack do you want, Alyssa?" Risa asked.

"Surprise me," I said, smiling.

She nodded and went over to investigate the machine's offerings. I sat back and put my arm around Paula, who was really looking out of it. The blood on the back of her head had dried, and her face was mostly cleaned up, but she needed to be cared for. I sighed with relief, feeling glad that Jacob had stopped at this hospital. We had been ill-equipped to handle our friend's injuries.

Looking around the Emergency Room, I saw there were only a few other people here, and no sign that the infection had touched this area of California. Indio was apparently so far out of the large city areas that it had remained unscathed. Before Risa could come back from the vending machine snack, a nurse approached me with Caitlyn. She performed a cursory exam on Paula, then brought a wheelchair over and we got her into it.

"You're going to be okay, Paula," I said, looking into her eyes. "These people are going to fix you right up." I straightened and nodded to the nurse, who wheeled Paula down the hall to be examined.

"Holly went in to get checked," Caitlyn said, sitting down.

"That's good. I hope everything's okay with the cut on her arm, and her baby and everything," I nodded, yawning and leaning back to stretch, my hands on the back of my hips.

I sat back down with Caitlyn, and we both yawned simultaneously. Laughing, we leaned against each other and rested. I saw the nurses bringing Mike in on a stretcher and stood up and went over to see what was going to happen with him. They wheeled him through the lobby and down into the hall toward the exam rooms before I could catch up with them.

"Hi, what's going on with Mike?" I panted as I jogged up to them.

"Not sure, but I think his leg is broken," DeAndre answered, stopping to talk to me with Jacob. The nurses wheeled Mike out of sight. We all went back to the waiting room.

"I should go move the van to a parking place and take the dogs out for some more exercise," Jacob said. I nodded and plopped down into a chair next to the others. Risa was back and handed me a cold soda. I took it thankfully.

"Thanks, Risa. This is actually perfect," I said, popping the top and gulping half of it down. It was so cold it hurt my throat and woke me up a little, which was wonderful. I pressed the can to my forehead and cheek. God, it felt so good to do something so normal. Risa climbed up to my lap, and Caitlyn dropped her head on my shoulder. My eyes drooped as I finished the rest of the soda. I quietly put the can next to me, wrapped my arms around Risa as she snuggled against me, and rested my head against Caitlyn's. We all promptly dozed off.

Sometime later, I heard DeAndre and Jacob talking nearby about Mike. Opening my eyes, I sat up and caught Risa as she began to slide off my lap. Caitlyn was sitting up as well and rubbing her eyes.

"Hey guys," I said quietly, yawning and stretching, "any word on things?"

"Yeah. The doctors said Mike's leg is broken and needs a cast," said Jacob. "They said Paula needed stiches and has a concussion. Her arm is being put in a cast, too. I think they said it was fractured in two places."

"They're both going to be discharged after they get their casts on. We were just discussing leaving them here in this town and driving on to Phoenix to find our families," DeAndre said.

I sat up, straightening my shirt and nodding, "I think that may be the best thing to do." I glanced around for Holly. "Is Holly still being seen?" I asked.

"I'm not sure," answered DeAndre.

"I'll go ask," said Caitlyn, yawning and stretching her arms above her head. She got up and ambled to the nurses' station, followed by Risa.

"Have you guys asked about the infection? Have they heard anything at all?" I asked, turning back to Jacob and Mike.

"I don't know," Jacob said. "This town is only about 100 miles from L.A. And it's on the direct route to Phoenix. They had to have heard something."

"Let's go ask," I said, getting up and taking Jacob's hand. We all went to the nurses' station and joined Caitlyn.

"Hey, we've just driven from Central California, stopped in L.A. and then arrived here," Jacob said, catching the attention of the two nurses and a doctor at the desk. "Fresno and Bakersfield had fallen to the plague and L.A., we found out, was severely compromised. Have you guys seen or heard anything about it out here? You're just a couple of hours out of L.A. and when we left he observatory we were being chased by infected individuals." "Wha?" said the doctor. The two nurses simply looked dumbfounded.

"Yes, that's about it, in a nutshell. The infected individuals all act like zombies. They attack people if you give them the chance," I said.

"Well," said the doctor, "of course we've heard about the emergency, but we haven't seen any cases of it here. I had no idea it had reached L.A."

"Oh, yeah. It's in L.A," I said. "That's why we're worried about Holly. She got infected blood and tissue all over her wound when she was attacked. We were running to our van, and a zombie jumped her. Jacob here took care of it, but, well, can you let us know how she is?"

"What do you hear about the evacuations coming down the 10 from L.A. to Phoenix?" asked DeAndre.

"We weren't aware of any evacuations just yet," said a nurse.

Just then, a third nurse came out from the exam room hallway. "Miss White will be out in a few minutes, the doctor is just finishing up running some tests on her. She seems to be doing okay," he said, writing on his clipboard.

"Well, I'm going to wait out here, stretch my legs," I said, gesturing to an enclosed patio with an open ceiling that was off to the side.

I opened the door and looked up at the sky, past a few large plants that were arranged around the patio. The black, inky expanse was gorgeous. There were so many stars this far out from the city, and they all seemed to be winking at us. I felt a renewed sense of hope regarding Holly's fate. And Mike and Paula were going to be okay, too. We were all going to make it out of this with just a few bruises and scars.

Risa ran off to try and catch a moth that had wandered into the patio. It was pure white and fluttered around her head as she laughed and tried to jump and touch it. Fluttering off, the little moth alighted on a leaf about 8 feet above the ground. Risa stopped right under it and gazed up, mesmerized by the little creature.

I smiled.

Jacob and the others joined me on the patio a few minutes later, holding sodas. Caitlyn handed one each to Risa and me, and we popped the tops and took long, deep swigs. The frosty liquid burned slightly as it made its way down my throat and into my stomach, but it tasted like heaven.

"I can't wait to get to Arizona and meet up with my family,"

DeAndre said quietly, drinking his soda.

"I know," I said. "I figure we should maybe get a couple of motel rooms for the night and then set out for Phoenix in the morning. I'm sure there're some nearby places. And we need to get some real food in us."

DeAndre nodded. "Sounds good, Alyssa."

Jacob came over to me and silently wrapped his arms around me in a gentle hug, laying his chin on top of my head. We stood there, swaying a little back and forth to some silent tune, for many minutes. I closed my eyes in bliss as he started to rub my back. A warm glow filled my heart.

Just then, the glass doors opened and Holly stepped out.

"Hey guys!" She said with a smile. We all crowded around her.

"How are you feeling, Holly?" I asked. Her arm had a neat white bandage around it, and her scrapes had been cleaned up. She smiled and held her belly.

"I heard the baby's heartbeat, it sounded strong. It was so good to hear!" she said enthusiastically. Risa giggled and patted Holly's belly, then hugged her. Holly hugged her back, smiling.

"Let's go check on Mike and Paula," I said to Jacob. He looked into my eyes for a minute, then leaned over and kissed me gently. He then took my hand and nodded to the others and we went back into the Emergency Room lobby, leaving a bemused group of friends behind on the enclosed patio.

Jacob led me up to the nurses' desk and asked about Mike and Paula. We were led back through the hallway and into the first room. Mike looked up at us, smiling.

"Hey guys!" He said.

The nurse turned to us, "I'm finished with him. He's all yours," she said smiling. To Mike she said, "Try to stay out of trouble, okay Mike?" He smiled and shrugged. She left the room to give us privacy.

"Mike, we're going to get rooms here in the city and then head to Phoenix in the morning. Do you want to stay with us and drive out? Or?" Jacob trailed off.

"I'd just as soon stay with you guys and drive out to Phoenix with you," Mike said, easing himself off the exam table and steadying himself with the crutches the nurses had supplied.

"Okay, sounds good. Let's go check on Paula," I said.

Moving on down the hallway, we found her room and knocked. The nurse popped her head out of the room. "Yes?" she said.

"Is Paula okay? Can we talk with her?" Jacob asked.

"Actually, I believe the doctor will be admitting her overnight. Her head wound is pretty bad, and she has a bad concussion. She's been vomiting," the nurse said.

Jacob wrote on a notecard and handed it to the nurse. "Can you be sure she gets this? It's our phone number. We'll be leaving for Phoenix in the morning," he said.

The nurse left the room and closed the door softly behind her.

"Are you sure you want to do that? She'll probably get discharged in a day or two. She'll want to see her relatives," the nurse said.

"Oh, no. We're not related to her. We just gave her a ride from Bakersfield," I said.

"Oh, I see. Well, I'll see to it she gets your number then," the nurse said, waving the card Jacob had given her as she re-entered the exam room. "Have a safe trip," she said as the door closed.

We walked back down the hall and out to the lobby, where the others were waiting, gathered around a T.V. set bolted up in the corner of the ceiling. It was airing a story about the plague reaching Los Angeles, and about how the evacuations of people from the north were set to continue into tomorrow. No mention of the chaos of the escaped zombies at the observatory.

"They probably don't want to start a panic," Caitlyn mumbled.

Just then the news reporter cautioned that people were advised to stay away from the Griffith Park area of L.A. and that police were being sent in to "control the situation."

"That's it, there you go," gestured DeAndre in disgust. "Now why don't they feel they can tell people *why* those police are being sent in? Censoring this information is just going to cost lives."

"I don't know," I said, shaking my head, "but it's not a good idea, that's for sure. Come on, guys. Let's get out of there and get something to eat. It's nearly 10 p.m., and I'm starved. Listening to this is just going to make us more upset."

"Alyssa's right, let's just go," said Holly, looking angry.

We headed on out to the van, piled in and drove down the road to a nearby restaurant called Maxcy's Grill. Once we were seated and eating, we started to relax a little more.

"I'm really concerned about the censorship going on with this infection problem," DeAndre said.

"Yeah, you can get more accurate news on Twitter than you can on a local news station about an epidemic," said Holly, "What are they trying to cover up?"

"I don't know, but remember the police barricades Coach Turner got us around when we were driving west? That was less than a week ago. And the situation getting out of control at Griffith Park. And the news censorship. Guys, I smell military action," I said.

"I would not be surprised if they tried to quarantine the whole state of California," Jacob said quietly, laying down his fork. "The military usually has the mentality of containment. And we've seen how well containment efforts work on a small scale. The Griffith Park Observatory situation was completely out of control."

"Do you really think they might try to quarantine the whole state?" I asked just as quietly.

"They might. They probably will," he said, looking at me.

We continued to eat in silence, all of us deep in thought. The meal revitalized us, and when we left the restaurant, we felt immensely better. We found a motel a bit further down the street, and got a couple of rooms and bedded down for the night, dogs and all. Before we all went to our rooms, we conferred in the parking lot.

"I think we should all meet at the van early. Say 6 a.m.?" Jacob asked. "That way we can get an early start. I have a bad feeling about this quarantine possibility, and I think we should get out of California as quick as we can."

"Agreed," Mike said.

"Yes, absolutely," chimed in Holly and Caitlyn.

"I say we try for 5 a.m., just in case," said DeAndre. The others nodded.

"Okay, 5 a.m. it is," I looked at my cell phone. "It's just before 11 p.m. now. Set your alarms and meet out here at 5. Have a good night. I know I will. Come on, girls, let's head to bed," I said, rounding up Caitlyn, Holly and Risa and heading for our room. Jacob, DeAndre and Mike all headed to the second room.

Chapter Eighteen

I was so exhausted I didn't even bother removing my clothes. After setting the alarm on my cell phone, I kicked off my shoes and fell back onto the bed. I think I was asleep before my head hit the pillow, curled up with Risa next to me on the king bed. Scooter and Blackie snoozed on the floor, snoring gently. As I dozed off, I could hear Holly taking a shower, then Caitlyn after her. I wondered how Holly's arm was, bandaged in the shower. Right before I slipped to unconsciousness my thoughts turned to Holly's baby. I imagined it faintly calling to me for help, through water and darkness …

I awoke to the quiet yet insistent beeping of an alarm drifting into my dream. I had been dreaming about a trapped kitten that was crying for help. Except the kitten wasn't mewing, it was crying out, 'Help me,' very faintly. I was searching for it, but so were some rats, and there were a lot of them, looking through rubble for this kitten. It was dark, and I could hardly see a thing. Then in the darkness, a faint yellow light grew, from just a pinprick, to a soft, dull glow, just enough to see by. I reached for where I thought the kitten was …

The alarm finally reached my unconscious mind and forced it to awaken. I groggily opened my eyes, vaguely upset that I would never save the kitten from the rats. Damned dreams, I thought.

"Alyssa, wake up," Caitlyn said softly. Holly was sitting up in bed and Risa was still asleep, tucked next to my belly. Was she the kitten?

I shook my head.

"I'm going to take a quick shower. What time is it?" I asked.

"About 4:30 a.m.," Caitlyn answered, yawning. I grabbed my backpack, got my toothbrush out and went to clean myself up. It would be good to be clean, I thought. I hoped I had a fresh t-shirt left. Behind me, I heard Caitlyn rouse Risa.

Stepping into the shower, I quickly lathered up my hair and body. The hot water steamed up the room and felt like heaven on my sore muscles. For a few minutes I sighed and leaned against the shower wall and just enjoyed the feeling of nothingness. After a while I shook myself and finished rinsing off. Wrapping a towel around my head, I emerged from the bathroom and found Holly and Caitlyn mostly dressed. Risa was jumping on the bed. Where did the girl get all this energy? Scooter and Blackie barked at Risa, and jumped up on the bed with her.

"Risa, go in there and take a shower, Sweetie. You stink," I said smiling, patting her on the back as she giggled and ran into the bathroom. I turned to the others.

"How're you guys doing this morning?" I asked. The shower had washed away the remnants of my sleep, and I felt energized.

"I feel great, but I want to get out of this state as soon as possible," Caitlyn said.

"Me too," said Holly. "I rebandaged my arm last night, and it feels fine. I just have this unsettling feeling in my stomach about staying any longer. I'm happy we're heading out this early."

"Your stomach?" I looked worriedly at Holly's midsection.

"No, no, ha ha! I'm fine. It's just butterflies," she said, patting her stomach, "Baby is doing just great. He kicked me half the night, but he's settled down now," she said with a smile. "I just want to get to

Phoenix ASAP."

Nodding in agreement, I gathered up my things and headed out the door to check on the van. Jacob was already out there, straightening up the back compartment that held our supplies.

"Good morning," I said, poking my head in next to his. "Want any help?"

"I'm mostly done, but thanks," he said, backing out and straightening up. He smiled at me warmly. "You look all freshened up!"

I smiled at him and leaned forward. "It's amazing what five and a half hours of sleep will do," I whispered conspiratorially to him. Winking and giving him a kiss on his cheek, I patted my stomach and added, "but I am famished for some reason. After that meal last night, I didn't think I'd eat for a week, now I want to stuff my face!"

Chuckling, he said, "I've got some granola bars and soda up front already."

"You saint!" I said, and went around front and grabbed a granola bar. Popping open a Pepsi and munching on the bar, I walked back to the room to check on the girls' progress. Caitlyn has Risa out of the shower and toweled off, and they were looking for a clean t-shirt for her.

"I think all your stuff is pretty filthy, Risa," Caitlyn said.

"Here, use one of mine, sweetie," said Holly, tossing Risa a small white t-shirt. Holly was a tiny girl, but still, the shirt hung down nearly to Risa's knees. Giggling, I ruffled her hair.

"Maybe we'll get a chance to do laundry soon," I said. She smiled up at me. I reached down and, going all around her waist, tucked the shirt into her jeans. "There now. That's better," I said.

Caitlyn and Holly had gathered up the dogs and everything, and we all headed out to the van. Mike and DeAndre were there, loading up.

"Jacob went to the motel office to check out, he'll be back in a minute," said DeAndre, taking the dogs out to a strip of grass off to the side.

I nodded.

"Mike, how do you feel?" Caitlyn asked as she tossed her bag into the van.

Mike hobbled over on his crutches. "I'm getting used to these things. My leg feels okay. They did a good job," he said, tapping the side of his cast with the rubber knob of the crutch. "Anybody want to sign my leg?"

"Ooh! I do!" chirped Risa.

We all settled into the van, Risa next to Mike, already drawing away with several markers.

I belted myself into the driver's seat and put the key in the ignition. Soon, Jacob came around the corner and hopped in beside me.

"Ready to go?" I asked.

"Yep," he answered, returning my smile. "Next stop, Phoenix, Arizona!"

Pulling out of the parking lot and onto the freeway, I let out a sigh of relief. Hopefully we'd find our families in Arizona. Maybe we would get some real answers to the questions we all had about this plague. Was there any hope for containment? How could they hope to fight an infection that spread so rapidly? Was there any cure for someone infected but not yet turned? And why did some turn so fast, within hours even, and others takes more than a day? A dozen more questions swirled around in my mind as I drove.

I had been driving for about two hours, chatting intermittently with Jacob as he perused the Internet for news of the infection. We were both becoming quite fond of each other, and sometimes, he'd lay his hand on mine as I drove, rubbing it softly. Then we became aware of some odd sounds behind us.

DeAndre came up to the front to inform us. "Guys, Holly's feeling a bit ill. Can we stop somewhere?"

"Sure, D. What's she feeling? Is it her stomach again?" I asked.

"I don't think so. I think she's having some contractions," DeAndre said. My eyebrows rose in alarm. Jacob unbuckled himself and wordlessly made his way to the rear of the van. DeAndre sat down in his vacated seat. He looked relieved to be up front.

"You okay?" I asked.

"Yeah. It's just that pregnant ladies make me nervous," he said with a laugh. "Holly looks about ready to pop. Then all of a sudden she clutches her middle and doubles over. Caitlyn was with her, and she seemed fine after a minute, but it was freaky. I've never seen a baby delivered. And she's so thin," he said, sounding worried. Scooter came up to him then and whined, and he rubbed her head.

"I know. She's had a lot of nausea. She said the doctor back at Kennedy told her she was underweight. But she didn't seem to eat much at dinner last night," I said.

Nodding, DeAndre said, "I noticed. She only ate about half of her dinner." He glanced behind him at the commotion in the back of the van and shuddered.

"What's going on?" I asked, trying to concentrate on both the road and the sounds coming from Holly behind me.

"I can't see too well. Caitlyn is beside her, and Jake and Mike are trying to talk to her. She's just kind of moaning every now and then."

I chuckled. "You sure are nervous, D," I said, smiling. Just then, Jacob came back up to the front. DeAndre got up to give him his seat, and then sat behind him instead of going back to the rear of the van.

"Holly seems to be having contractions. She thinks they might be Braxton Hicks contractions. You know: those practice ones they get toward the end of their pregnancies?" Jacob said. I nodded. He continued, "but they seem pretty painful for just practice contractions. I think maybe we should stop for a bathroom break and maybe get her something for the pain. Tylenol or something," he finished.

"Okay," I said. "Sounds reasonable. I think there're some gas stations coming up in a few miles, I saw a sign, and we need to fill up anyway."

After a few more minutes, I took the exit and pulled into a truck stop/gas station/minimart setup. Jacob hopped out and hooked up the gas pump. Caitlyn and I helped Holly out and headed to the bathroom. Risa hopped back and forth, asking questions like, "Is Holly going to have her baby here in the gas station?" which made Holly give her looks of disgust.

I laughed.

"No, sweetie. Holly is just feeling a little sick. She'll probably be just fine in a little while. Why don't you go with Mike and pick out a snack, okay?" I said.

"Yeah, kiddo. Come with me, let's stay out of Miss Holly's way. I think I'm going to get some Twinkies!" said Mike. At that, Risa squealed and ran ahead into the minimart. I looked gratefully over at Mike.

"Thank you," I said.

He smiled. "No problem. I hope Holly's feeling better soon. If there's anything I can do…" his voice trailed off, and he looked mildly helpless.

I smiled. "I'll let you know," I said, and then he walked off to join Risa and we headed into the hallway to the bathroom.

In the bathroom, Holly immediately headed for a stall and stayed in there for quite some time. Caitlyn and I finished and washed up, then we waited for her outside in the hallway.

"Do you think she's going to be okay?" I asked.

"I'm not sure. She was feeling some bad pain in the van. She looked kinda worried," Caitlyn said.

"Hmmm…"

Just then Holly emerged from the bathroom, looking very pale.

"Oh my God, I just threw up so bad I thought I'd see the soles of my feet in the toilet, guys," she mumbled.

"Holly, are you going to be okay?" I asked. She looked strange. Her face was paler than ever. She looked white as a sheet.

"I think so. I feel better for the moment. I think I just need a cold drink, maybe just ice water. My stomach just can't hold down much right now. This feels like it did my first trimester. I couldn't keep hardly anything down for weeks."

"Well, come on. Let's see what kind of drink we can get you," said Caitlyn, taking her by the hand and leading her around the corner and down the hallway. I trailed behind, lost in thought. I was trying to remember how it was for my mom right before she delivered my baby brother. I wondered if Holly was going into labor.

After a while, it seemed clear that she wasn't. Her contractions seemed to have stopped.

"Alyssa, they have Ding Dongs!" said Risa, bouncing up to me happily.

"That's great, Sweetie. I think I'll just get an energy drink and some chips, though," I said, ruffling her hair. Grabbing a can and selecting some chips, I went looking for the guys. I found them at the end of the store, putting way too many condiments on questionable looking hotdogs.

"Hey guys," I said as I walked up next to Jacob. "Hot dogs, huh?"

"Yep. Breakfast of champions," said DeAndre, smiling. "Want a bite?" He lifted his onion-covered hotdogs up to my face.

Laughing, I pushed his arm away. "Actually, it looks pretty good, but I think I'll just stick to these chips for now. I'm never very hungry in the mornings," I said, smiling.

"This sweet pickle relish is going to go great with all the onions," Mike said, ladling mounds of the green mixture onto his hotdog. I looked over at Jacob, who was creating a chilidog with cheese dribbled on top.

"Ewwww!" said Risa as she sidled up to my side. Her hands held her Ding Dong and a package of Twinkies.

I laughed. "Not quite you're taste, huh kiddo?"

Risa shook her head, wrinkling her nose at the sight of the boys' hotdog creations.

I laughed and headed to the register to join Holly and Caitlyn. Holly had opted for a cold iced tea and some crackers. After paying for everything, we headed out to the van again. The sun was just starting to break through the morning mist. I lifted my face to catch the yellow warmth and sighed. Looking at the van, I saw how worn it was getting.

"Risa, want to help me wash the windows, kiddo?" I asked. Risa smiled and ran to grab a squeegee. We spent the next few minutes trying to make a dusty windshield into something resembling clean. Risa went to the back and wiped off the rear windshield some.

"I'll finish that up, if you want," said Jacob, returning with Mike and DeAndre. He smiled at me and put his hand around my waist softly. A shiver of delight ran up from my toes to the top of my head and made the hairs on the back of my neck stand up.

"Sure," I said, turning to him with a smile. He lowered his head and kissed me lightly on the forehead, then rubbed my back.

"Go get in the van, I'll take care of the rest," he said.

Smiling dreamily, I got in the driver's seat, and Risa hopped in after me. I saw Caitlyn and Holly exchange smiles.

"What?" I said to them.

"Nothing, nothing at all," said Holly.

"Alyssa, he really likes you," said Caitlyn, smiling.

I smiled back and looked out the window at Jacob cleaning the windshield in his white t-shirt. My eyes were drawn to his biceps and his muscular back and shoulders. I sighed.

"He's a pretty wonderful guy," I said softly.

"Who, who?" chirped Risa. Scottie let out a "yip!" beside her.

"Nobody, Sweetie," I said, turning back to the dashboard and absently dusting off the console. A few minutes later, everyone was back in the van and we were headed back onto the eastbound freeway. Jacob was again up front next to me, looking up information on the iPad, and Holly was dozing in the back with the others, feeling better. I had a feeling of relief, I certainly didn't want her going into full-blown labor in the van. I felt a strong urgency to get to Phoenix, not only to reunite with our families, but to get Holly to a hospital where they could check her out again, and find out what had caused those hard contractions.

"There's not much coming out of Los Angeles," said Jacob. "I think they may have gotten things under control."

"That's good news. Twitter is not going crazy with tweets about zombies then?" I asked.

Jacob shook his head. "Hardly anything, really. And I think they got the entire San Joaquin Valley evacuated, there's really no news coming out of that area, not like there was last week."

"Any news on any government quarantines of California?" I asked.

"No, but I wouldn't expect that to be leaked anyway," he said.

"What about the evacuations from L.A. to Arizona? All those buses leaving Griffith Park for Phoenix. Any word on those?" I asked.

"Let me check," he answered. He tried a few different hashtags and Google searches, then:

"Hold on. Okay, here's some news. It seems like everyone who was bused out of Griffith Park was definitely taken to Phoenix, but they ended up at several different locations in the city. It looks like there are at least three different large hospitals in the Phoenix area: St. Luke's, Banner and St. Joseph's. Plus there are lots of motels, hotels, and school auditoriums. They may have scattered when they got there. I'll check if there's any place where there's a bulletin board or something."

I drove on, worrying thoughts filling me head. I just wanted my mom and little brother to be safe, wherever they were. And I wanted to be with them. As if on cue, "Reunited" by Peaches and Herb started playing on the radio and made my eyes tear up. I switched it off in disgust, and continued driving on in silence. Jacob looked at me questioningly, but I stared straight ahead at the road, blinking my eyes clear again. My mom and little brother were fine, and I would see them soon, I kept repeating in my head. No need to worry at all.

Chapter Nineteen

We were a little more than an hour out of Phoenix when Holly doubled over in pain. I heard her gasp and looked back and saw her clutch her belly as it spasmed. Jacob went back to help, and even DeAndre stayed back there. I sped up a bit and raced on. Jacob had given me directions to St. Joseph's Hospital, and I hurried to get us there. I hoped Holly would be able to last that long, but from the sounds coming from the back of the van, I wasn't so sure. Then Jacob came to the front of the van.

"Alyssa," he said, not bothering to sit down. "Holly's face and hands are turning light grey."

Oh my God! No! I pressed down on the accelerator until we hit nearly 90 mph and hoped there weren't any police in the area.

"Tell me what's going on. From the sounds of things I thought she was having more labor pains," I said, trying to keep a note of hysteria out of my voice.

"I think she's infected. She is having labor pains, but her skin. Remember how pale she was when we stopped?"

I nodded.

"Well," he continued, "she's white as a sheet, and near her ears and neck, and at her fingers, her skin looks like it's getting slightly greyish. Her labor pains are about 10 minutes apart, but they are hurting her. And you can even see her middle contracting. I think we need to get her to the hospital as fast as we can."

"I'm going over 90 miles an hour. I think we have about an hour's drive to go. Try to make her comfortable if you can," I said. He nodded and started to turn back toward the rear of the van.

"But Jacob," I stopped him. "Get some rope, just in case. If she turns inside this van, with so many people in such a closed compartment…" I trailed off, looking up at him.

He nodded grimly. He knew it was a death sentence for us all if that happened. He went to check on Holly again and I turned back to my driving. The chips and soda I had eaten earlier began to make me feel nauseous as my stomach cramped with stress. Oh, God. Holly. Her baby. My eyes teared up again, and I made no move to wipe them. Grimly, I drove on, racing against an infection that was sure to kill our friend, and her unborn baby.

Holly's cries were getting worse, and I still had about 50 minutes to go.

"Alyssa, she can't last. Can you pull over, please?" Jacob said quietly right behind me, making me jump about a foot. "I'm sorry, it can't be helped. The movement of the van is making it worse, and I think she's getting greyer."

"Sure. Absolutely," I said, swallowing hard and pulling the van off the freeway, onto a side street and into a small parking lot. I stopped it and took the keys out, locking the doors as well. Jacob and I made our way to the back of the van.

Holly was stretched out on the back seat, her face covered in sweat and turning a combination of grey and red. Her eyes were full of fear.

"I'm infected, aren't I?" she said, her voice shaking.

"Holly, just take it easy. We've pulled the van over. Just concentrate on your baby," Caitlyn said gently as another spasm took hold of Holly. Her head lifted in pain as her midsection seemed to clench with the contraction. As it receded, Holly began to cry softly.

"Just tell me, okay? I have a right to know!" she said.

Jacob leaned forward and looked into Holly's eyes.

"Your face is turning grey, Holly. That's all we really know so far. You seem to be acting normally, like a woman in labor. We don't know what's going to happen."

"We're here for you, honey," I said to her.

Risa squeezed her way between Jacob and me with a small, wet towel.

"I found some water, Holly," she said as she spread the little washcloth over Holly's forehead. "There you go," Risa patted Holly's head and smiled at her.

"Thank you, Risa," Holly said, smiling. Her smile twisted into a grimace as another contraction hit her. It seemed to last several minutes before it let her go, and she fell back panting as her body relaxed again.

"Alyssa, Caitlyn."

We leaned forward.

"My baby. I want my baby to survive," she said.

We didn't say anything. We didn't know what to say.

"Jacob," Holly said, grasping at Jacob's shirt front. He leaned in to her face.

"Please, save my baby. Please." She fell back as another contraction began to take hold of her. Her face turned red as she fought the pain. After another minute, she relaxed.

"Listen. Please. My baby. I don't care what happens to me. But take care of my baby. He deserves a chance," she whispered. She looked exhausted.

Her face was turning greyer by the minute. I looked down at her arms and legs. They were even darker than her face. I gulped and looked at Jacob, and then down at his hands. They held the coiled rope, half behind him, but at the ready. I looked back into his eyes and nodded slightly.

"Holly, I promise to take care of your baby," I said, looking into her eyes. "I give you my word."

A look of relief washed over her face, then a look of peace. Then another contraction seemed to take hold of her. She doubled over in pain, and a whimper escaped her mouth. She stayed like that for several minutes, doubled over and grimacing. Then she fell back against the seat.

"Thank you," she whispered. "His name is Luke," she said, and then she seemed to pass into a state of semi-consciousness. Her eyes rolled back into her head, and she fell back, breathing hard.

"Christ," Jacob said quietly, as he brought the ropes up and tied her hands together and then tied her up so she wouldn't be able to really move. He tied her head back so she could breathe, but firmly enough that she could not reach forward to bite anyone. Then we waited.

It didn't take long.

In less than ten minutes, Holly came to again, but it wasn't Holly that surfaced. Her eyes opened and they were bloodshot red, and a low growled issued forth from her mouth.

Her body bucked as she tore at her bindings, growling even harder. As I watched her middle, I could see it spasming again and again as it fought to push the baby out.

"Hold her, okay? This baby has to come out," I said.

Jacob nodded, and he and DeAndre managed to position themselves at Holly's head, holding her shoulders and torso down as best they could. Caitlyn and I positioned themselves at her legs, which had been tied down as well. Mike held Risa up front.

Caitlyn and I lifted her dress and pulled down her panties. Her legs spread wider, as far as the restraints would allow. I looked up at Holly's eyes once more and was surprised to see them mostly clear.

"Promise me again, Alyssa!" Holly said, able to get this one last sentence out before turning completely.

"I promise, Holly," I said.

Her face then turned upward and she let out a scream like no other. It began as a normal scream then changed into a howl and then a loud growl. She seemed to be howling in rage against the unfairness of life. She had to get infected and turn into a zombie and die, right at the moment that her baby was born into the cold world that was becoming impossible to live in.

I looked down at her and saw the baby's head had crowned. With another howl and spasm, the baby's shoulders popped out, first one, then the other. A moment passed and then he slid out, hot and steamy and wet, into my arms. And Holly growled and raged at the heavens.

I wrapped the little baby up in a blanket Caitlyn had handed me and held him to my shoulder, my arms curled around him protectively as his mother screamed her rage at the sky. The placenta slipped out, and Caitlyn wrapped it up into the blanket, too. Another howl filled the interior of the van. Looking back up at Holly, I saw her face was turning a dark grey, her eyes were going milky, and the last vestiges of the person she had been were gone.

"Get out!" yelled Jacob. "The ropes are slipping! Get out of the van, everyone!!"

Mike had open the side doors, and we all piled out like ants boiling out of an anthill. I turned and jumped, clutching the baby to my chest protectively. My feet hit the pavement, and I straightened, looking back. The dogs rushed past me. Everyone was out of the van except Jacob, who was trying to control Holly.

"Jacob!" I screamed. I was so terrified that he would get bitten.

He finally turned and jumped out himself, slamming the van door shut behind him, and we ran to the far end of the parking lot. Holly was still in the van, growling and fighting her restraints. She was nearly free of them.

"The shotgun is still in there, dammit," Jacob said, watching the van rock back and forth with Holly's thrashing. Suddenly, she threw the door open and fell out sideways and I saw that her feet were still tied together. She kicked at the restraints madly, and we all backed further from the van. It was mesmerizing to watch. Her face, arms and legs had gone almost black, they were such a dark grey.

Suddenly, a police cruiser pulled over next to the van and an officer got out. He didn't see Holly at first, and approached us.

"Are you people okay?" he asked. We mutely shook our heads and pointed back at the scene next to the van. Holly was still kicking violently and had nearly gotten her legs free. The police officer turned and jumped at the sight. Drawing his gun, he slowly approached Holly, who was still down on the ground. As he got closer, she screamed like an animal and kicked her legs free of the ropes Jacob had tied. Scrambling to her feet, she growled and advanced on the officer.

"Watch out!" Mike yelled.

"Oh my God ...," Caitlyn said.

Holly got within five feet of the policeman, growling like an enraged animal, before he emptied his gun into her. The first shots hit her in the torso and knocked her back to the pavement. But after a few seconds, she growled and picked herself up again and began to advance on the officer again. I heard him gasp.

"What the hell?" he said in amazement. Then he shot her again in the chest. It would have put any normal, living creature down for good, but Holly just stepped back a few feet and turned again toward the policeman. Her milky eyes were rimmed with red. Red blood ran down both legs, not from the shots fired into her, but from the birth of her baby. Her blood had stopped pumping after the birth and before she had been shot. She took several more steps toward the officer, and he backed away from her. He was clearly dismayed, but his training clicked in and he didn't panic. He pumped a third shot up higher, this one hitting her in the shoulder. Holly spun around halfway and stumbled. But then she got her footing and again advanced on the officer.

We were all watching this with amazement. Our friend had turned into a zombie and was taking gunshots at close range that were barely slowing her down. She weighed all of 120 pounds soaking wet. But now she was tougher than a bull.

The officer's gun rang out a fourth time, this shot going over her shoulder as she ducked. She was learning. In the short time the duel had been occurring, she was learning. I watched, incredulous, as I held the baby close to me. I took a peek at his face and saw his mouth was open and he was crying softly. I patted his back and soothed him as another shot rang out in that early sunny afternoon on the side of the street just outside of Phoenix, Arizona.

The officer's fifth shot hit Holly square in the face, shattering her nose and part of the forehead as it drilled into her brain. It stopped her in her tracks, and she fell backward. It all seemed to happen in slow motion. Blood, almost black, and brains spewed out from the hideous wound, as her body hit the ground. Pieces of her brain were splattered behind and below her head. Her face was half gone, and she looked like a crumpled little zombie doll, covered in bullet holes.

And definitely dead.

Chapter Twenty

The police followed us in our van as we drove to the hospital to have Holly's baby checked out. News had spread to them about the plague infection, and several evacuees had turned after arriving in Phoenix, but this was that officer's first personal experience with a zombie. His fellow officers, who arrived a few minutes after he called for backup, had to calm him down to get the whole story. Then they questioned us all, at the scene, thoroughly, before letting us go.

We all ended up at the hospital, where doctors checked the baby out. He had still been inside her when she had turned, but only just barely. We didn't know if he had been infected, too.

Jacob presented himself as the baby's father, so they would let us keep him after they were done examining him. I had made a promise to Holly, after all.

On the ride to the hospital in the squad car, I studied the baby's face. His eyes were tightly closed, and his face was red, but I was looking for signs of the plague. I looked very closely, and I couldn't be sure, but it seemed like his face was slightly greyish. I worried years off my life on that ride to the hospital.

After they had examined him thoroughly, and knowing what had happened to his mother after he had been born, the doctors weren't sure what to make of Luke. That was what Holly had wanted him named. Luke. And we had granted her that last request.

After he was cleaned up, examined, fed, washed, warmed, vaccinated, and clothed, Luke looked normal. And he acted normal, too. They kept him under observation for several days, but he appeared to be healthy. He weighed 6 pounds, 11 ounces. He ate well. Everything was perfect. And they had no reason to hold him there.

After three days, Jacob and I walked out of St. Joseph's, followed by Risa, Caitlyn and DeAndre. I cradled Luke in my arms as we walked out into a warm, sunny, normal day. It was surreal.

We stayed at a motel for a week, figuring out what to do, gathering baby stuff and equipping ourselves to take care of a newborn. Diapers, formula, little outfits, blankets. All the while Risa never stopped hopping from foot to foot in her excitement.

"A baby!" she kept exclaiming. We just smiled. We were all still so sad about Holly, but Luke distracted us all. He was a very good baby. He ate well, and slept most of the time and hardly cried at all. He brought a little joy into a sad world.

Mike had moved on to find his cousins, and we dropped the dogs off at a no kill shelter. It was, once again, us kids, on our own. We tried to find news of our families, who had supposedly been evacuated to this city, but they wouldn't tell us anything. So we waited.

Eventually, we learned that most of the busloads of evacuees had come to a bad end. One or more of the passengers had turned, most on the trip here. The buses had either crashed or become entirely infected. Hardly anyone had survived. My mom and little brother, my grandparents: all gone. I never found out which bus they'd been on. But after searching for a month, making dozens of calls and visiting each evac site, I came to accept that I would probably never see them again.

It was much the same for Jacob, DeAndre and Caitlyn's families, as well as Risa's. We even tried to find Emily's parents, but to no avail. The authorities were pretty tight-lipped about the whole thing, too. They presented us with lists of the surviving evacuees, but none had our relatives on them. It was a sad time, made happier only by the presence of Baby Luke.

We kept looking for signs of what they were going to do about the plague. After a while, the military stated they had the situation mostly under control. Two days later, however, there was another announcement that California was *not* under control, and that travel into the state had been halted. It seemed the infection had not only spread from Palo Alto to San Francisco and Fresno and Bakersfield, and to Los Angeles, but to San Diego as well. Mexico had sealed off their border and wasn't allowing anyone into their country. The Mexican army had stationed guards along the border for a hundred miles.

We stayed in the motel for that first week, trying to prepare ourselves for what we knew was coming. And come, it did. But in a form we weren't expecting.

"Alyssa, come here," said Caitlyn. She had been feeding baby Luke with a bottle in a chair. Jacob and I had been talking quietly nearby. Okay, we had been mostly gazing into each other's eyes. But there had been a few words. I think. When Caitlyn called me over, Jacob and I both got up and went to her.

"What's up, Caitlyn?" Jacob asked.

"How's our perfect baby doing with his breakfast today?" I asked, smiling.

"Look at Luke's face," Caitlyn said quietly.

We looked down and both of us went silent. DeAndre came in then, from the outside hallway. He had been changing the oil on the van and he wiped his hands with a rag as he walked in.

"What's up, guys?" he asked, walking up to us all. We were silent. He looked down at baby Luke, held in Caitlyn's arms. Luke gurgled quietly and let out a gentle burp.

We all looked down at Luke. We were struck with silence. We looked at that baby, disbelieving.

Luke's face was light grey.

Acknowledgement

A huge thank you to Steve Provost for his support and editing expertise.

ABOUT THE AUTHOR

Samaire Provost lives in California with her husband and son.
Her love of paranormal stories, odd plots, and unique tales as well as the works of Neil Gaiman, Terry Pratchett, Susan Cooper, Madeleine L'Engle and Stephen King has deeply influenced her writing.
This is her first novel.

19128616R00096

Made in the USA
Lexington, KY
07 December 2012